Sky Rider

Sky Rider

NANCY SPRINGER

AVON
tempest

AVON BOOKS, INC.
1350 Avenue of the Americas
New York, New York 10019

Copyright © 1999 by Nancy Springer
Interior design by Kellan Peck
ISBN: 0-380-97604-8

Library of Congress Cataloging in Publication Data:
Springer, Nancy.
  Sky rider / by Nancy Springer.
  p. cm.
  Summary: Dealing with her mother's death, a back injury that prevents her from riding, and the imminent destruction of her sick horse, fourteen-year-old Dusty receives physical and spiritual healing from the ghost of a recently killed boy.
  [1. Horses—Fiction. 2. Ghosts—Fiction. 3. Death—Fiction. 4. Angels—Fiction. 5. Future life—Fiction.] I. Title.
PZ7.S76846Sk 1999   98-52303
[Fic]—dc21   CIP
                                                          AC

First Avon Tempest Printing: July 1999

AVON TEMPEST TRADEMARK REG. U.S. PAT. OFF. AND IN OTHER COUNTRIES, MARCA REGISTRADA, HECHO EN U.S.A.

Printed in the U.S.A.

FIRST EDITION

QPM 10 9 8 7 6 5 4 3 2 1

www.avonbooks.com/tempest

Sky Rider

Prologue

Daily SouLog Anno Domini 1998, 4th moon, 17th day
Subject Skye Ryder, young male American, death recent, untimely and unfair. Subject is having trouble with transition. Vengeful anger is holding him back from ascent, puts him in danger of soul death. A latent gift of telempathy has kept him out of ultimate peril for the time being; however, he remains in the physical vicinity of his death site. Subject appears immobilized in so-called ghost phase. He is, in effect, "haunting." Subject must undergo transition if he is not to remain indefinitely imprisoned in ghost phase—or worse—but sector supervisor is reluctant to suggest intervention, as subject cannot achieve full soulhood unless he chooses it for himself. Maintaining watchful care.
J.G., Sector Supervisor

Chapter One

"No, Tazz," Dusty whispered as the tall bay gelding nuzzled her hip pockets, "no more carrots." Hugging his neck, with her face in his black mane, she wanted to cry but joked instead. Dusty always joked when life got not funny at all. "Too many carrots will make you sick," she informed her horse gravely. "You don't want to get sick for Doc, do you?"

It was dark in the stable, shadowy in the light of a single forty-watt bulb. At dawn the vet would come to put Tazz down. Euthanize him.

Kill him.

Dusty blinked hard, let go of Tazz, bent over—moving stiffly because of her back brace—and picked up her sisal cloth. Tazz loved to be curried. All night Dusty had been brushing him, rubbing him, sweet-talking him. He stood in the stable aisle with no halter on him, no cross ties, not even a rope looped around his neck. Dusty knew he would not bolt out the open door. As she rubbed his red-brown crest, he lowered his head with a sigh that fluttered his soft nostrils. He stood with his ears at a contented sideward angle. With his big eyes half-closed.

With one forefoot extended because of the navicular disease.

In a moment he shifted his weight and stretched the other forefoot, trying to relieve the pain. The great-hearted thoroughbred who had once borne Dusty over Olympic-size fences, who had raced goldfinches on the wing for the fun of it, who had run bucking down the pasture every morning just because the sun was up, could no longer hobble more than a few steps at a time. Tazz lived in constant pain.

Dusty knew what intractable pain was like. Her back hurt all the time now.

Like Tazz's forefeet. Once the navicular bones in his hooves went bad, there was no cure, and no treatment except painkillers—which had stopped working as his condition got worse. But even with Tazz barely able to walk, it had been hard to make the decision to end his misery by putting him down. "Remember, Dusty," her father had told her, trying to help her accept what had to be done, "Tazz doesn't know, so he doesn't dread it. He won't be frightened. It's not like we're sending him off to the auction or the slaughterhouse. It'll just be Doc, right there in his own stall. He won't care."

Yes, Daddy. But I care.

She tried to stop thinking about it. Didn't want to cry till this was over. Didn't want to scare Tazz.

"*Big* show, Tazz," she whispered owlishly as she picked up the soft brush. Let him think she was grooming him for hours and hours to get him ready for Devon or the National, like in the old days when she would be busy in the stable hours before dawn, when he and she, Miss Destiny Grove riding Razzle My Tazz, had won trophies all up and down the east coast. Back before her stupid spine got hurt and she couldn't ride anymore.

Out of nowhere, out of the 3 A.M. silence came a sudden chilly wind and, in Dusty, a gale of anger. *Why don't they just put me down too? I'm unsound. I'm costing a lot of money. I'm in pain, I'm useless, why don't they kill me?* "Tazz," she cried, throwing down the brush, "nobody should die young!"

The gelding's head jolted up, but not because Dusty had startled him. With his ears pricked high he was staring beyond her, toward the rectangle of night outlined by the big stable door. She turned.

There had been no sound of a car or a bike or even a footstep, but a stranger, a boy maybe sixteen years old, stood there looking at her.

Dusty felt her world stop, she was so startled, even frightened—yet she did not scream. He was too beautiful, a white marble Michaelangelo in Levi jeans, shadows softening his chiseled face. There was something not quite human about his beauty, yet something all too hot and human about the way his dark eyes glowered. He kept his face hard and still. The anger showed only in his eyes.

The breeze had halted as if the night were holding its breath. Nothing moved. Nothing made a sound.

Then the boy moved, one swift step toward her. He spoke. "You want me to take him?" His fierce, soft voice resonated between the stable walls.

"Huh?" Dusty couldn't think. His shadowed stare wouldn't let her think. What did he want? What was he talking about? Who was he?

"For God's sake," he said even more quietly, more fiercely, "it's either me or the vet. You want me to take him?"

He was talking about . . . Tazz? He seemed to be. His dark gaze had turned to the horse, and his hard face softened. His hot stare gentled momentarily as he walked to Tazz and lifted his hand to stroke the silky fox-red cheekbones, the white blaze between deep, wise eyes. Dusty stood still. For once she couldn't think of a joke—but Tazz would tell her what to think of this stranger. Tazz knew things. All horses did.

When the stranger touched him Tazz did not shy away. His ears alerted so high that they almost touched at the tips, quivering. He tucked his chin, arched his shining neck, snorted—but not in fear. "Holy *gee*," Dusty whispered, for in Tazz's eyes she saw a blue fire she had not seen there for a couple of years. Morning was coming, and Tazz wanted to leap right over the sun. He rose into a low rear and came down with his weight squarely on his forefeet as if they had never heard of pain.

"You want me to take him?" the boy demanded again, not turning around.

Tazz reached with his head toward the boy. "Yes," Dusty whispered.

The boy glanced at her with a look she could not read. "Fine." His voice was as hard as his face, and she began to wonder whether she had done the right thing. "Let's see whether I know how to ride a horse."

With a couple of quick, sharp strides he positioned himself at Tazz's side. "I guess I can only get killed once," he said. Grasping the long, black mane, he vaulted onto Tazz's back.

Tazz flung up his head and neighed like a golden bugle. Again he neighed, long and loud, quivering all over and stamping his forefeet in his eagerness to go, run, fly. The boy grabbed the mane with both hands and leaned forward. Tazz whinnied, plunged his head, and lunged into a gallop within a single stride, bursting out of the barn as if out of a starting gate.

In the days to follow, whenever she thought she couldn't handle all the crazy things that were happening for even a minute longer, Dusty would close her eyes and remember Razzle My Tazz's vast, leaping joy, replaying it like a movie in her mind: Tazz, cantering across the stable yard and jumping the pasture gate with a foot to spare and high-tailing it across the pasture and jumping the fence even more extravagantly. Tazz, bucking with sheer moonlit euphoria—and yes, the boy did know how to ride, he sat on the big red horse like a silver flourish placed there by the wide-eyed moon. Then Tazz, with the boy swaying along with his every jubilant move, Tazz galloping to the crest of the hill, kicking at the stars—then gone in the night, out of sight.

"Whoa! What happened?"

Blinking into the darkness, Dusty found that her feet had carried her across the stable yard and halfway across the paddock, and that her father was standing barefoot and pajama-bottomed beside her.

"What's going on? What spooked Tazz?"

Tazz wasn't spooked; couldn't he see that Tazz was wild with joy? But Dusty did not correct him. With her mouth still agape, it was all she could do to get out a couple of words. "The boy," she whispered.

"What boy?"

"The boy . . ." She found that she could not describe the boy who had appeared out of the night. What was she supposed to say? That he had a face too perfect for a human being and eyes like burning coals and hair as black as Tazz's mane? That he had come out of nowhere and healed the horse with his touch? That he was either a devil or an angel in white T-shirt, ripped jeans, sneakers? "The boy riding Tazz. . . ."

"When? Somebody rode Tazz?"

Dusty turned to her father, staring. "Just now!"

"Huh?" He stared back at her.

"Didn't you see him?" How could he not have seen? "A boy—" An indescribable boy. "A boy I don't know. He touched Tazz, and . . ." Dusty faltered, thinking of her horse, of his transformation, his exaltation.

Her father's stare gentled. "You were dreaming," he told her softly.

"No, I wasn't."

"Yes you were. You must have been. There wasn't anybody here."

But . . . but . . . Her mind stuttered. Her sleeping bag lay spread on some hay bales in the barn, unused; she knew she had not been dreaming. More like screaming. She had yelled something and turned around and the boy . . . Why hadn't her father seen the boy? Dusty asked, "Did you just catch the tail end?"

"No, I didn't catch any tail end. I wish somebody would have caught his tail end. Goofy horse."

"Tazz is not a goof!"

"Yeah, well, anyway, I woke up when he neighed. I saw the whole thing."

"You saw him take off like a rocket?"

"Yes, I saw him. More like a wild turkey. Why are we standing here arguing about your dream?"

It wasn't a dream, Dusty wanted to say, but she was getting the strangest feeling, like silver feathers brushing her spine, sending shivers through her. Feathers of silence. She stood staring at the far hills, not saying anything.

"Are you okay?" Her father peered at her.

"I'm fine."

"Your back hurting you?"

Of course it hurt; it always hurt. Dusty shook her head.

"Well, we've got to get moving. Catch Tazz. What spooked him so bad, anyway?"

Dusty said nothing.

"You had him loose in the barn, didn't you?" Her father's grumbling was gentle. Dad knew she had been agonizing about Tazz. Maybe he even suspected that she had somehow made Tazz run away herself, although it would have taken a firecracker under the tail to get Tazz to run these days. Daddy should know that. Maybe he did, because he dropped it, or handed it back to her. "Any idea where to start looking?"

"I'd just wait a while. See if he comes home on his own." She knew he wouldn't.

Her father shook his head. "You can stay here if you want. I'm going after him." Typical, Dusty thought. Daddy was a classic Type A. He had to do things, mess with things, try to make things happen; he couldn't just let things go, not ever. He was sweet, but when he got something on his mind it was like he had bugs in his ears: you just couldn't make him listen. Like now. He turned away and stomped off toward the house to get the car keys, wincing as his bare feet hit stones under the grass.

Dusty stood where she was. She took a deep breath of cool nighttime air, listening to the darkness, scanning the indigo pastures. The moon was setting over rumpled hills she had known all her life—she saw nothing out there to make her tremble. Yet she stood quivering, feeling the silent touch of invisible wings.

There was a boy.

A boy who—who shone like white fire.

He was here. I saw him.

Bang! The slam of the house door startled her. Daddy came out, wearing shoes now, keys glinting in his hand. "Maybe I can find him before old Nisley sees him and starts trouble," he yelled to Dusty as he got into the Bronco four-by-four. The next moment he roared up the lane.

Dusty rolled her eyes. "You're the one who started trouble," she said, knowing her father could not hear her; she would not have said it to his face. But she often thought it. The way her father had been feuding with the neighbors the past couple of years made no sense to her. So what if the Nisley boys and their friends biked through the woods now and then? Dusty had ridden through Nisley land back when she could actually ride and the Nisleys had crossed Grove land and nobody cared. But Daddy had changed.

Dusty sighed. Since Mom had died, everything had changed so much.

It was an aneurism, but it might as well have been the sky falling. One day Mom was fine. The next day Dusty got called out of class. The vice-principal drove her to the hospital. By the time she got there, Mom was already gone.

The evening after the funeral, Dad had several

drinks to help him sleep. He'd always liked a couple of drinks before dinner, to help him relax, he said. And he'd always enjoyed drinking at parties, getting a bit happy. But now almost overnight he was drinking, not because he liked it, but because he needed it. He would get home from work and start drinking and just keep going. When Dusty asked him to stop, he said he would but he didn't. Even when she told him she needed him to talk with in the empty evenings, even when she just about made him cry, he couldn't seem to stop. After the first few weeks, he got angry if she said anything about his drinking. Sometimes he drank so much he passed out.

Dusty's friends tried to help her after Mom died. They hugged her in school every day, called her every night. But somehow Dusty couldn't tell her friends that her father had turned into a drunk. He was all she had left. She didn't feel that she could tell anybody, even when he started drinking earlier in the day, even when he started drinking and driving.

It was the accident that had shocked him into sobering up, started him going to AA. That had been a bad time, only six months after Mom died, and the doctors telling Dusty that her back was never going to be right again, and Tazz getting worse all the time—but time helped her get used to the way things were. And Daddy started going to AA, so in at least one way things were better now. Dad was almost like the old Daddy now that he was sober—well, maybe a bit more of a control freak than he used to be. Somehow he'd gotten this idea that everybody had to stay off his land. He was almost paranoid about property lines. Before *Nisley* started trouble, he'd said? Old Mr. Nisley wouldn't do anything bad if Tazz strayed onto his land.

Dusty took a deep breath and one more long look at the indigo night. Tazz was out there. But somehow she knew her father would not find a tall, red horse wandering on the country roads. She had a feeling that the stranger boy was riding Tazz to a place far removed from Grove land or Nisley land or the world as she knew it.

The feeling reassured her. Tazz was somewhere safe. Yet, it . . . scared her.

In a daze, she wandered into the barn and lay down on her sleeping bag, barely noticing that her back hurt atrociously, her mind in a kaleidoscope swirl of Tazz, Tazz, Tazz and the inexplicable boy. Tazz as he had been the past couple of years, a little more lame every day, until the hard decision had been made—but now Tazz rearing up with the blue fire of joy in his eyes again, Tazz leaping as if he wanted to fly, Tazz running to the sky. The boy with shadowed eyes appearing out of the night. The boy . . .

Better not tell anyone about him, Dusty decided. She did not want people talking about her behind her back, the way they used to talk about her mother.

Tazz saw the boy, too. That means he's real, doesn't it?

Except . . . Mama had always claimed that horses saw spirits. Dusty remembered one time when she was a little girl riding Pinocchio, her first pony, with her mother beside her on a palomino mare: the pony had spooked hard at an inoffensive white oak tree. "He saw a ghost," Mom had said. "A hundred years ago a circuit preacher tied his horse to that tree and a panther got it. It was a wall-eyed piebald horse. Pinocchio knows." At the time, Dusty had taken it seriously, that when horses spooked for no apparent reason they were seeing spirits. Then when she got older she had decided that her mother had been kidding her. Now she was fourteen and it was starting to look like her mother had not been kidding her at all.

The boy. What had he been doing there? The Grove place was way out in the country. People didn't commonly appear there at any time, let alone at three in the morning. How had he gotten there?

And how had he known what was wrong?

What was he? He was too eerily beautiful. Her heart was beating too hard just thinking of him. She was too grateful. Why had he healed Tazz? And how?

Would Tazz be all right with him?

Who was he?

An angel, her mother would have said. An angel without wings. Mama had talked with angels regularly. Other than that, she was a normal mom—no, she was a great mom. Washed breeches, packed tack, braided manes better than anybody. Rooted for Dusty from the sidelines of every show. Knew just what to say whether it went well or not. World's best organizer and world's best hugger. Mom had some oddball opinions about angels and things, that was all. Dusty swallowed hard, missing Mom all over again even though it had been almost two years since—since people stopped calling Mom eccentric, because it wasn't nice to speak ill of the dead.

Eccentric? Maybe not. Maybe Mom knew something.

Or maybe it was too scary to think about. "Okay," Dusty whispered, blinking into the shadows. "Okay, whatever." In the rafters overhead, the swallows were starting to stir and twitter in their nests and okay, soon the sun would rise and somewhere, Dusty hoped, Tazz would nicker and buck and chase butterflies. She knew what she had seen. Her heart raced every time she remembered. But she would tell no one. Normal people didn't see such things.

Chapter Two

Dear Diary,

It's Sunday night April 19 and for some reason Daddy is really a grouch. I'd like to talk to Katelyn but he won't even let me use the phone. I would like to whack him on his pointy head but I can't so I'm hiding out in my room and I guess I might as well write in you for a change.

It's been a strange weekend. Friday night real real late I fell asleep in the barn, finally, and Daddy just let me lie there and sleep all day Saturday, which was sweet of him. Which was why he had scheduled the vet to come on a Saturday morning in the first place, so I'd have the weekend to regroup, so I wouldn't have to go to school right afterward or anything, except the vet didn't have to come after all because Tazz took off—or that's what Daddy thinks. He says he called the police and the radio and all that, but nobody's seen Tazz. I have a feeling Tazz is better off, so I'm glad. Sort of. Or at least I'm not upset. But Dad doesn't understand, so he is fussing. He jumps like a cat every time the phone rings, and he won't let me answer it. Saturday night I was wide awake after sleeping all day so he rented a bunch of videos and we watched them till three in the morning, which was nice. Then I slept till noon today, and then Daddy took a notion that we had to go out for dinner and a "Sunday drive," so we did. We drove clear to Maryland and back and we didn't get home till after dark. But then all of a sudden Daddy got totally squirrely. He won't let me turn on the radio or the television and there are messages on the answering machine but he says they're all private for him and he can't sit down, he's pacing by the phone. He's a mess. I would like to take him and shake him. Finally I told him to chill out and then he *really* got crabby. I wish he wouldn't get like that but then I remember how it was when he was drinking and I realize it's a lot better to just let him grouch. So here I am in my room and I'm not tired but I guess I might as well go to bed. Nothing else to do. Homework, what's that? Anyway, I have a first period study hall tomorrow.

P.S. Diary, I turned off the light to go to bed but then I kept looking out the window. There's nothing out there except hills and woods and moonlight and shadows and the mares and old Pinocchio in the paddock, but I kept staring like I couldn't help it. So I've turned the light back on and I'm going to sleep that way. Aaak. I guess I'm more upset than I thought.

On her way to school Monday morning, watching as her father drove the Bronco, Dusty thought that he looked too tired, seemed too quiet. But she didn't say anything. Didn't want to get snapped at.

"Look," he said suddenly as he pulled up in front of Grovesburg Intermediate School to drop her off, "honey, you have a *good* day, okay?" It was almost like a plea, which was not his usual style at all.

She tried to make him laugh. "Daddy, I have other plans." But he didn't laugh, and the look on his face made her say, "Daddy, what's the matter? Are you okay?"

"Yeah, I'm fine. See you, honey." He drove away. A man in an expensive three-piece suit driving a dusty four-by-four to his downtown business. For just an eyeblink Dusty saw him, really saw him as if he weren't just her father, and what she saw was a man with too many obligations. Abel Grove. As in grandson of the Abel Grove who had founded Grovesburg. As in C.E.O. of the plastics business that kept the town going. A civic leader and executive who probably would rather have been a farmer. It was kind of sad.

Then her glance shifted across the blacktop to the high school, and she stared. In front of the big doors, two girls who looked like they might have been juniors or seniors were hugging each other and crying. Several more were standing close together without talking, and they were all wearing dresses. Some boys stood farther apart, somber and quiet, wearing suits or jackets. Gray, black, navy.

"Dustin!" sang a voice that made Dusty smile and turn. Katelyn seemed to come up with a new nickname for her every time she saw her.

"*Pierced* nails?" Dusty asked, her glance caught by Katelyn's rhinestoned frosted lilac fingertips.

"No, just glue-on studs." Katelyn stepped closer, apparently with a more serious subject on her mind. "Listen, Dustbuster, I tried to call you to see how you were and everything." Because of getting Tazz put down, she meant. "But your dad said you didn't want to talk."

"That's dumb. Of course I wanted to talk." Good grief, what was Daddy trying to prove? What was wrong with him?

"He sounded stressed. Was it real bad?"

"Actually, it sort of didn't happen." Rather than try to explain right then, Dusty looked back toward the high school. "What's going on with the dresses and everything?"

Katelyn lifted her studded fingernails in a kind of salute. "They're going to the funeral, I guess."

"Funeral?"

"Didn't you *hear*, Density? Where have you

been? Some high school boy got killed over the weekend. The funeral's today."

Before Dusty could react, another friend, Lauren, came up. "Dusty! I heard your horse is lost!"

"Yes, but—"

All that day at school Dusty tried to explain to one friend or another that Tazz was gone but it was okay; if he had not run away he would be dead. Talk of Tazz, Tazz, Tazz mixed with talk of the boy who had died—"No, got killed," Dusty thought, vaguely realizing there was a difference. Killed how? Car wreck? Ew. She didn't like to think about car wrecks, so she didn't ask. "One of the Ryder boys," somebody said. She had heard of them a little. Wild, handsome boys. She felt both glad and sorry that she hadn't known the dead boy. Glad because she didn't really have to deal with this. The pills she took for the constant pain in her back made her woozy some days, and this was one of those days and she had trouble concentrating on anything. "Caught him right on the neck," she heard in the halls. "He was going about forty." Dusty didn't know where the boy had wrecked, or how, and she didn't get to ask because friends kept asking her about Tazz. They knew how much she adored her horse; they had been horrified and sympathetic when she had told them that she and her father had decided that Tazz

23

needed to be put to sleep. But now Tazz was out there somewhere. "What happens when you get him back?" Katelyn asked.

"I—I'm not sure." Dusty found that she could not explain, not even to Katelyn, why she was not worried, why she felt sure it would not happen. She could not say anything to her friends about the eerie boy's appearing in the night; she just couldn't. They wouldn't understand. Mom would have understood, but Dusty could not think of anybody else who might.

It's all right, Dusty thought. Some things were best kept to herself. *I can handle whatever*. If she just didn't feel so tired and woozy. Her head felt so cottony that she couldn't think.

Getting off the school bus, every part of her as weary and achy as her spine, Dusty saw the Bronco parked in the driveway. Odd; why was Daddy home already?

She went into the house. "Daddy?"

No answer.

She dumped her book bag on the kitchen table, and then she saw the bottle.

"Uh." The sight hit Dusty like a punch to the stomach. Whiskey. Or rather, it used to have whiskey. Now it was just glass, open and empty. She stood staring at the smelly thing, feeling herself go wooden.

She tried to lighten up, tried to think of a joke. But she couldn't. This was just not funny. Daddy had been doing fine for the past year, going to AA and keeping his promises. What could have happened to start him drinking again? This Tazz hassle? Dusty didn't think so. It had taken a lot— the shock of finding his wife unconscious and dying—to turn Daddy into a drunk.

"Daddy?"

No answer.

"Oh, *Da-a*-dee." She could allow herself the sarcastic sing-song call because she knew he wasn't a mean drunk. He had never been a mean drunk. Just . . . pathetic, that was all. Slurring, slobbering, runny-nosed, lugubrious. A pain in the butt.

Dusty sighed, and slowly, because she dreaded what she was going to find, she went looking for him.

Still in his business suit, he lay passed out face-down on the living room floor with another bottle close at hand. He hadn't puked; his head was turned to one side and it looked like he was breathing okay. Dusty knelt down and put a hand on his side to make sure. Then she stood up, took the bottle, and left him where he was.

In the kitchen again, pouring whiskey down the sink, she felt her weariness harden and go stony, a cue that she was deeply angry. But it was no use being angry. She knew she ought to make some phone calls, get Daddy's AA buddy out here, try to find out what went wrong, try to get Daddy back on track. But she didn't feel like she could deal with it yet. Maybe after she found something to eat.

She headed for the cupboard where she and Daddy kept the peanut butter. A newspaper was lying on the countertop. She glanced down, and everything stopped.

He was looking back at her. The boy.

His photo. On the front page.

It was him, the boy who had healed Tazz and ridden off into the night. She would have recognized him anywhere. Yet . . . it was not exactly him. The boy in the picture—he was handsome, but . . . human, normal. Real. But the boy she had seen in the night—it was as if someone had taken this boy and polished him like glass and filled him with white light and black fire.

Skye Ryder, the caption said. AREA TEEN KILLED, the headline said.

The Ryder boy. The boy everyone was talking about in school.

Shakily Dusty reached for the newspaper to pick it up and read the article.

The phone rang.

She crossed the kitchen to answer it. "Hello?"

"This is Nisley," said a gruff voice. "Yer horse is up here."

One crisis at a time, Dusty told herself as she headed out the door. *Just take it one crisis at a time.* Story of her life. *Dad will wait.* She knew from experience that he would lie on the floor quite a while longer. *So will the newspaper.* It was not likely to levitate from the countertop where she had left it. *What's Tazz doing back? Is he okay?*

Her heart was pounding in her hurry to get to the neighboring farm. Briefly she thought of grabbing the keys and taking the Bronco. She knew she could do it, though she had never driven on the road, only around the farm. But if a cop happened to catch her on the road, she would be in big trouble. And even if nobody caught her, she knew she couldn't hitch up the trailer by herself, let alone tow it, so how would she bring Tazz back?

Did she want to bring him back?

No. If he was lame again, she would hide him somehow, somewhere. But she tabled further thought about that decision until she had seen him. With a lead rope tied around her waist and a halter hanging on her shoulder, she set off on foot, short-cutting across country toward the Nisley place.

It had been a long time since she'd tried to walk so far—less than a mile, but her back started to hurt before she even got across the pasture. Dumb, that after all the dangerous things she had done on horses, polo and steeplechase and jumping bareback and trying to stand on the horse at a canter like a circus rider, after all that, her back had been totaled not by a fall from a horse but by her own dear drunk father swerving into a ditch when she was in the passenger seat. The forty-mile-an-hour jouncing had done compression damage to her spine that the doctors were never going to be able to fix. Just the way they had tried every kind of vet and medication and corrective shoeing for Tazz, she and Daddy had tried doctor after doctor, treatment after treatment, for her back. After a year and a half, it looked like pills, pain, and back braces were going to be her life.

As quickly as she could, while little black-and-white Pinocchio and two chestnut mares watched her curiously, Dusty trudged past the pasture pond and up the hill to the gate. Had it really been more than a year since she'd been out here? It hurt to remember what she had felt like back then, with Mom dead and Dad in treatment for his drinking and Tazz dead lame and her back— well, her wrecked-up back had felt like one damn thing too many. Story of her life, she had told herself at the time. What was the use of even wanting things to be any different? But now, at the sight of the familiar hilltop, her chest squeezed with yearning.

Oh, to ride again. She remembered everything vividly. Same makeshift fence-wire gate. On the far side of it, same maze of grassy trails between blackberry thickets. Tiny blue-white flowers in the grass. Tiny blue-white butterflies flying up in clouds. Lump in her throat—that was new. She hadn't realized till now what this particular piece of Eden meant to her.

More than a year. Why hadn't she walked out here before?

Well . . . because she didn't feel like doing things, that was why. Everything hurt. More ways than one.

Still, Dusty lifted her head as she reached the woods, smiling at the tall hickories and tulip poplars, the dirt trail like a wide, lazy river winding under them, a brown meander rippled with footprints, hoofprints, bike tire tracks.

She walked into the woods, breathing deeply, ignoring the pain in her back. Good old trail. How many times had she cantered along here? How many times had she fallen off, trying to get a balky, bucking pony to change leads? It was a soft, safe trail. Safe landings—

Abruptly she stopped walking and stared. Something had changed.

Across the trail at her feet, someone had dug a

ditch about a foot wide and six inches deep. A ditch lined with spikes. Rough-cut steel railroad spikes. Points up.

Nasty.

And ugly. And *stupid*. Suppose a horse stepped into that? Or a person?

Who would have dug such a mean thing?

Without answering her own question, Dusty stepped over the ditch and trudged on. Suddenly she felt very tired and very conscious that her back was screaming. It was no longer a pleasure to walk along this trail. All she could think about was getting to Nisley's. She felt like she had no energy to think about anything else.

She came to another ditch lined with spikes. This time she walked around it. Judging by the narrow side trail worn through the ferns and mayapple, other people had been doing the same. The ditch had been there for a while. How long?

Just keep walking. Don't think. Don't think about . . . pain.

Something bright yellow caught her eye. Up ahead. She walked more slowly, staring, then faltered to a halt.

Glaring yellow plastic tape stretched from tree to tree, enclosing an area about ten feet square, blocking the trail. POLICE LINE DO NOT CROSS, it said. POLICE LINE DO NOT CROSS.

Step by hesitant step, as if something might hurt her, Dusty inched closer until she almost touched the tape. But she could see nothing to tell her why it was there. Maybe somebody else could have made sense of the marks on the trail dirt, but she couldn't. Or the marks on the trees. Twin hemlocks flanked the trail, and on each of them the bark was scarred about four and a half feet above the ground. Dusty saw nothing else.

Tazz. She had to get moving. Stop thinking about things that didn't concern her. Go to Tazz.

Picking her way between deadfalls and saplings, she made her way through the woods until she was past the obstacle. Back on the trail, she tried to run. Ow. Owww. Couldn't do it. Panting with exertion and pain and frustration, she pushed herself along at the fastest walk she could manage. Almost to the road—

There was a gate barring the trail from the road. A red metal gate. That was new, too.

As with the ditches, people had worn a narrow side path to get past the gate. Dusty followed it out to the road, a rutted gravel road Daddy never drove her along, good for horseback riding and bike riding but not for girls with bad backs. Another place she hadn't been in over a year, Nisley's road. She stood looking back at the padlocked gate across the trail head. PRIVATE PROPERTY, a metal sign proclaimed in black-and-red letters. KEEP OUT. THIS MEANS YOU. The *O* of *you* was painted like a bull's-eye.

Dusty shivered.

Well, yeah, it was private property. It was Grove property. The edge of her father's land, which would be her land someday. *And when it's mine,* Dusty thought, *I'll tear down that sign and that gate and watch the kids on ponies ride through.*

She would sit on her stupid back porch in her stupid brace and wave as the kids on Welsh Arabs rode by. And they would wave back. So would the kids on dirt bikes. It would be a lot better than sitting there and looking out on lush land with nobody enjoying it.

I'm not even going to think about who put up that stupid gate.

She knew who. She knew who obsessed about trespassers all the time lately, as if putting up gates could give back some sort of control over a life that had gone wrong. She knew who had been calling lawyers. Writing letters to the newspaper. Fighting with the neighbors.

Dusty thought of the ditches with spikes in them, then pushed the thought away. One crisis at a time. Tazz first. She headed down the road toward the Nisley place.

Chapter Three

"Where's your father?" old man Nisley said in that gruff way of his. "Ashamed to show his face?"

"He's not feeling well."

"Too sick to drive?" Nisley did not sound sympathetic. "He let you walk over here?"

Dusty stood up straight in his farmyard and tried not to show how much her back was aching. "Flu," she said firmly, then changed the subject. "You say my horse is here?"

"Yep. Sashays in like he's looking for something." Nisley flapped one of his big hands toward the old red barn squatting at the bottom of his lane. "I'm in the barn, and he skips in like he wants to confabulate with me, and I just shut the doors."

Nisley spat tobacco juice onto the gravel. "He's in there. You kin go catch him."

Dusty found that she had to know before she saw Tazz. "Did he act lame or anything?"

"Lame?" The old man blinked. "Nah. Looked pretty frisky to me."

"Thank you." It came out a whisper. Trying to walk strongly, Dusty headed toward the barn.

"How you getting him home?" Nisley called after her. "Can't that father of yours bring the trailer over here? You call him, tell him I'll stay in the house."

Dusty had to smile at the old man. "I'll just ride him home," she called back.

"You can ride?" Nisley was right to be surprised. He knew about her back.

"That little distance, sure. No problem." Actually, the idea had just that moment occurred to Dusty, and it set her heart pounding. Ride Tazz, ride her horse once more, now that he was no longer lame? She would probably trash her back royally—but it already hurt so much, who cared? She would ride Tazz one last time instead of leading him home. His mane would stir with each step. His ears would prick eagerly as he carried her along. His warm shoulders would flex under her hands. Even if it put her in the hospital, she would ride.

She pushed the barn's heavy sliding door open just enough to slip through. Inside, it was so shadowy that for a moment she could not see. "Tazz?"

"He's busy trying to chew us a way out of here," said a sardonic voice.

Dusty stiffened and stared. Seated cross-legged in a wheelbarrow, the eerily beautiful boy stared back at her.

"Skye," Dusty whispered. She knew his name now.

He flinched and scowled. Dusty could not take her gaze away from him; his was a face fit to make an angel jealous.

She whispered, "You're dead."

"No *duh*." From the tone of his voice, he did not like being dead. Not one bit.

Dusty didn't know what to think, what to do, what to . . . What did you say to a kid who had died? Condolences? Maybe it would have been easier if she had known him when he was alive. Maybe not. She blurted, "Mr. Nisley didn't tell me you were in here."

"Like he can see me?"

Skye Ryder's obvious scorn was a little hard to take, but Dusty had a feeling he hadn't always been obnoxious. Being dead had to put a person in a really bad mood. Feeling awkward, she stood in a silence filled with the racket of Tazz's teeth on wood. She could see her horse now, big Tazz standing squarely as he gnawed at the rail of a cow stall. Somebody, probably old Mr. Nisley, kindhearted in spite of everything, had put a flake of hay and a few ears of field corn on the barn's dirt floor for the horse, but Tazz seemed not to have touched his snack, more interested in reducing Nisley's barn to splinters. Dusty said, "When he was little we used to call him Termite."

It was as if light had come out from behind clouds. Skye Ryder actually smiled.

Somehow the smile gave Dusty permission to function. She got herself moving. "Hey, Tazz!" He lifted his head from his wood sculpting to give her a horse's inscrutable stare, and she slipped the soft rope halter onto him. "Doofus," she murmured, "what do you think you are, part beaver? What are you doing here?" She led him over to the door, slid it all the way open and led him outside. He walked with the long, swinging stride of a strong thoroughbred, his forefeet drumming the ground in an easy rhythm. With not a trace of a limp.

"I rode him here," said Skye's hard voice. "I thought maybe this guy was the one. But if he was, he'd be feeling guilty. Haunted. He'd be able to see me."

Dusty stood without any comprehension of what Skye had just said, none at all, because glancing toward the sound of his voice, she saw him walk right through the barn wall to stand beside her.

"But . . ." Words failed her. She had been assuming that Skye had been shut into the barn like the horse, though that was stupid. Skye had hands. He could have slid the door open.

Or could he?

"What I can't figure," Skye said, "is how he can see the horse if he can't see me." The boy patted Tazz on his sleek red neck, rubbing his crest; Tazz leaned toward him, loving it. Skye's voice softened as he said, "Tazz is in the same kind of limbo I'm in."

Dusty blurted, "You were staying with him?"

His eyes flared like hot coals. His face hardened. He didn't answer.

Dusty turned away from his anger, her own stupidity. Of course he had been staying with Tazz.

Whose horse was this? His or hers?

She shied away from the question. *Later*—she'd answer it later. After her ride. She had promised herself one last ride.

"C'mon, Tazz." She led the horse to stand beside a rusting John Deere. Moving slowly and stiffly, she climbed onto the tractor, then onto Tazz, trying not to remember the days when she would have vaulted onto him, saddle or no saddle, from the ground. Then she sat light-headed, disoriented, it felt so strange yet right to be on his strong, warm back again. She gathered her single rope rein, turned her thoroughbred toward home, then stopped.

She looked at Skye. Standing on the ground, he tilted his chin defiantly upward to look back at her. His black eyes were burning. Anger. But along with the anger, mostly hidden by it, Dusty thought she saw some other emotion.

She held out her hand to him, silently offering him a boost onto the horse, a ride along with her.

His eyes went wide and still. His face went soft and still. Then he stepped forward and took her hand.

She saw. But she felt no contact, none at all. She saw him swing up onto Tazz right behind her. Or rather, one moment she could see him swinging up, and the next moment she could not see him at all. And she could not feel him sitting against her back.

"Skye?" she whispered, spooked. "You there?"

"Of course I'm here." His scornful voice sounded right behind her ear.

She swallowed and nudged Tazz into a walk. The big bay gelding strode easily, eagerly up the lane—and every step he took jounced Dusty's spine from side to side and sent a jolt of agony through her.

She concentrated on not showing the pain. Too much pride. Waving good-bye to Mr. Nisley, she smiled, showing her clenched teeth. Gripping the rope rein hard, she guided Tazz onto the gravel road, focusing on keeping each breath from hissing. She didn't want anybody to know how much she was hurting.

"What's the matter?" Skye asked, none too gently.

And she had thought she was hiding it so well. The sudden question made her blink back tears. Damn, she had wanted to enjoy this ride. "My back—hurts—so bad." The words came out ragged.

"What from?"

"Stupid—accident."

Skye didn't say anything. Dusty had no way of knowing what he was thinking behind her, whether he was moving, what he was doing, but just as she turned Tazz onto the forest trail the pain lifted away from her as if it were a metal sheath someone had torn off. She gasped. The sudden wellness, the release, filled her with a sensation as if she had wings; it snapped her head up, swelled her chest. Tazz felt her seat change and sprang into an airy canter.

"Better?" Skye grumbled.

She couldn't answer. As she leaned into her

horse's rocking gait, her throat was so tight with happiness that she couldn't speak.

"Slow down, for God's sake. We're coming up on the place where I died."

She felt so afloat with gladness that this did not trouble her. She did what he asked; she slowed Tazz to a walk, but all the time she knew she was crazy, none of this could be happening, and therefore nothing mattered terribly much. Almost as easily as if she were talking about last night's TV show, she said, "I don't know how you died."

"It was—there."

She did not feel surprised to see the gleam of yellow police tape through the trees. It was the place that had scared her earlier.

"Somebody strung a cable across the trail." Skye was having a lot harder time talking about this than she was. "Black. It blended right in. Four feet up, not down low like it should have been to stop tires. I was on my dirt bike, and I was wearing my helmet and chest protector and everything, but it—" He couldn't say it, but Dusty remembered from school. *Caught him right on the neck.*

She thought how it must have been. Riding along, fast, wind in his face and sun on his shoulders, young and strong, glad to be alive, and then . . .

Silently Dusty guided Tazz through the woods,

40

around the place where the killer trap had been. She no longer felt glad to be alive. The world no longer felt like a good place.

"I saw it a second before it got me," Skye said very low. "Just a streak of white sheen. Pretty. Spiderweb, I thought. You know how spiders put strings across the trails and they only show up when the sun shines a certain way."

Dusty nodded. She knew. "I used to love riding out here."

"So did I. Bikes are the best. But I can't ride bikes now."

Listening to him, Dusty guided Tazz around the first ditch booby-trapped with nails. The narrow side trail grew thick with baby striped maples, but Tazz did not snatch at any of the tender leaves within easy reach, not one. He was being an angel horse. Back when he was alive, Dusty had tried every way she could think of to keep him from grabbing "snacks." It was really embarrassing to ride into a show ring when your horse had a two-foot length of hollyhock dangling in glorious pink bloom from his mouth.

Back when he was alive?

"I can't work the gears or the handlebars or anything," Skye was saying. "My hands go right through them. But Tazz—it's different. He sees me, he feels me, he knows I'm riding him."

Dusty guided Tazz around the second ditch. The horse walked smoothly past another little candy-striped tree. Dusty asked Skye, "Has he stopped eating?"

"Yes. Same as me. He was meant to die, so . . . the other night, when I touched him . . . he—he crossed over. He's a ghost now, like me."

The G-word hung in the air like a specter. Beyond the ditch, Dusty eased Tazz into a gentle jog trot. She was trying not to think, just to enjoy the feel of riding along the woods trail and not hurting. Tazz tucked his chin and snorted. Maybe he was remembering, too, how it had been back when she was a kid and he was a strong young colt.

"I know he's still solid," Skye said, "but I think he's going to turn to light soon."

Dusty sensed that he did not usually talk so much. He seemed to think he had to convince her. But maybe because she was her mother's daughter, she had no problem believing what he was saying. It was something else he had said that seemed wrong.

Silent, Dusty lifted Tazz from his trot into a collected canter again. Out of the woods, into the sunshine. Down the hill along the grassy trail between blackberry thickets. As the downward slope steepened, she brought him back to a walk. Her heart ached with joy and sadness.

She told Skye, "You're not a ghost."

"Huh?"

"You're not a ghost. You—" This was hard to say, scary, way too much like something her mother might have said, but she made herself say it anyway. "You feel when people are hurting. You help people. You came to help when Tazz was going to die. You healed Tazz; you've healed me." Her heart swelled with gratitude for what he had done, and she felt sure that the gift had come to her on invisible wings. She just knew. With soul-deep certainty she said, "You're not just some kind of spook. You're a . . . you're an angel."

Dead silence for a moment. Then Skye said in a strangled voice, as if a hard rope had closed around his throat, "Stop this horse."

But Dusty had already drawn Tazz to a halt, gasping, the pain in her back closing on her like an iron garment she would wear for the rest of her life. She could not ride another step.

Skye said, as harsh as hail coming down, "I don't want to help people. I don't want to heal people. I just want to get the son of a bitch who did this to me."

"It's *gone*." Dusty could barely squeeze the words past her pain. Healing was gone. Joy was gone. "No. Please—" But she stopped herself from whimpering at him.

He demanded, "Who owns that land? Where I got killed."

"No-nobody." Stiffly, struggling, Dusty swung her right foot over Tazz's neck, sat sideward on the horse for a moment, then slipped down. The grassy ground, spongy with spring rains, gave her a soft landing, but even so, the pain of the impact weakened her knees. She sprawled, then managed to sit up. Above her, the spirit of Skye Ryder sat hard-faced and inhumanly beautiful on Tazz—sunlit, shining Tazz—looking down at her.

He said, "I need to know."

She shook her head. "Just take Tazz and go."

"I—"

"Just go away!" Suddenly she was shouting at him. She struggled to her feet and pulled the halter off Tazz. "You've got my horse, don't you? Get out of here!"

He didn't move. "Are you going to be okay?"

"What the hell do you care?" Staggering with pain, she turned her back on him and trudged toward home.

All the way across the pasture, feeling the warmth of Tazz's head on the halter in her hand, she did not look back. She heard nothing, no hoofbeats—but when she reached the house, let herself in, and looked out a window, Tazz and Skye were gone.

Chapter Four

D<small>AILY</small> S<small>OU</small>L<small>OG</small> A<small>NNO</small> D<small>OMINI</small> 1998, 4<small>TH</small> <small>MOON,</small> 20<small>TH</small> <small>DAY</small>
Subject Skye Ryder, recent ghost in danger of soul
death. Hopeful signs include (1) his attachment to
a horse he has rescued, and (2) his considerable gift
of telempathy—subject has discovered his healing
touch. However, his rage continues to negate his
healing power, while he remains unaware that this
is happening. Also, even on horseback, he continues
haunting behavior, refusing to travel more than a
few miles from his death site, thereby spurning the
possibility of ascent. Subject is suffused with rage
and appears intent on revenge for his untimely
death. At this stage, subject lacks the vision and per-
spective to see that the cable across the trail was

not intended to kill him or anyone else, that it was placed there by a troubled man who was not thinking clearly, who hoped that the booby trap might dump a trespasser on the ground, nothing more. In his anger, subject lacks sufficient compassion to accept that ego and stupidity, not evil, caused his death. Subject is too intent on his own pain to perceive the pain of others except, occasionally, that of the girl Destiny. She may well be his best hope. Continuing watchful supervision.

J.G., Sector Supervisor.

Dusty phoned Katelyn just because she badly needed to talk with somebody. "That boy who died," she told her, "the Ryder boy . . . that happened on my place. Up in the woods."

"Yeah. I tried to call you when I heard."

Everybody knew, then. "Why couldn't Daddy just tell me?" In her heart Dusty knew why, but she tried to feel only annoyance, which was safe. "He must have found out when I was asleep in the barn Saturday. Why'd he try to keep it from me?"

"Well, I guess he didn't want to, you know, upset you—"

Katelyn's answer sounded so lame it made Dusty mad. "Well, I *am* upset!"

"No duh. What do you want me to do about it, Dustbuster?"

The question made Dusty laugh. There was nothing Katelyn could do about Daddy, and Dusty knew it. They talked about other things; it felt good to chatter about dumb stuff, the leather jacket Katelyn wanted, fingernails and how Lauren had gotten her navel pierced. Katelyn wanted to get a second hole in her ears, but her parents wouldn't let her. After a while Katelyn said, "You want to do something? Go to the mall?"

"No. I can't."

"Why not?"

"Daddy's lying on the floor drunk."

"Oh, my God."

"He's passed-out drunk." It made Dusty feel better to say it, so she said it again in a different way.

"God. Dusty, I'm sorry." Katelyn knew Dusty's father was an alcoholic, and she could be trusted not to tell the whole world. "What are you going to do?"

"Use his butt for a coffee table, maybe. I don't know."

"Who can you call? His doctor or somebody?"

"His AA buddy. I will, then. I have to work myself up to it."

Katelyn was silent for a minute, then said, "I guess we both know what made him start drinking again."

"Yeah."

"You going to talk with him about it?"

"I don't know."

"Has he said anything about, you know, Skye?"

"No. I don't know a thing except what I read in the newspaper article." Which didn't name names, but it said that the police had questioned the landowner, which would be Daddy. Probably Saturday morning. According to the paper, Skye had died Friday evening, a little before dark.

When he . . . when he came to the barn, saved Tazz—he'd only been dead a few hours.

Probably Daddy hadn't known a thing about it then, and Dusty hoped he'd forgotten about her "dream" of a strange boy riding Tazz.

"I am so pissed," she blurted.

"At your father?"

"Yes." Actually more disappointed than angry. Hurt. Daddy had let her down so badly—

No. *No.* Daddy hadn't done anything to her except let her sleep all day Saturday.

And keep her away from the phone.

And get drunk.

"Dusty . . ." Katelyn hesitated, then asked softly, "Do you think he did it?"

"I . . . I don't know." The question panicked Dusty.

"Sometimes guys can act kind of stupid," Katelyn said. "Do you think maybe your father might have—"

48

"I said I don't know!" Damn, now she was yelling at Katelyn. "Sorry," she muttered. "Listen, I've got to go."

"No you don't. I'll shut up about it. Don't go stomping off, 'Buster. We can talk about something else."

They talked about hair, homework, Katelyn's new clogs. After a while Dusty said ciao and hung up and wandered to her bedroom. She felt better after talking with Katelyn, but Daddy was still snoring boozily on the living room floor. Dusty wished her mother were there. Mom would have known how to make Daddy get up off the floor and clean up and shape up.

Dusty stood at the window, looking out into the deep blue shadows of the night. With an ache that filled her chest she missed her mother.

Mama . . . Okay, it was all hypothetical, because Daddy hadn't been a drunk when Mom was alive, so maybe even Mom wouldn't have been able to make Daddy stop drinking. *Or make my back stop hurting.* Not even if she rubbed it with her warm, quiet hands. But if Mom were there, at least there would have been real meals—roast chicken with hot cranberry sauce, pot pie, beef soup simmering all day long, filling the house with its warm, brown, onion-and-parsley smell. There would have been daffodils on the table, maybe, and Mom smiling and asking how her day had gone and also talking with invisible spirits with names like Peri and Rabdos and Raziel, having these long discussions about things like What color was time? Could she give somebody her soul to keep in a jar like a firefly? If she could see forever, and the universe was curved, could she see the back of her own head? Sitting at the table and trying to include Dusty in the conversations as if she were translating or something. She would have included anyone, like it was only common sense good manners, but most people backed off. They thought Mom was cracked. But Dusty thought of her mother's quiet hands arranging the daffodils, adding long, aspiring leaves and jonquil and narcissus, placing them all just so in the tall amethyst vase, and she found nothing cracked in the memory.

Dusty sighed.

After a while she drifted to her diary to tell it the things that she could have told Mom but could not tell Katelyn.

Dear Diary,

I met up with Skye today, Monday, after school. I guess it's no use pretending anymore that there isn't a boy, that I'm not seeing spirits, or at least one spirit, the way Mom did. It's scary to be so different. I wonder if it scared Mom.

I read the newspaper article. It says the cable crushed Skye's throat and the shock stopped his heart and he died instantly. That helps some, I guess, that it was quick. But he remembers dying—I know he does—and that must be awful. He is so angry he's practically spitting fire. I mean, like what happened today. First he fixed my back and then he got mad and took it away. Talk about rotten attitude. I would like to take him and—I don't know—put him in a back brace or something. If he had to gimp around the way I do, he'd learn some patience. But at the same time I have to think, whoa, I'm alive and he's dead. I mean *dead*. As in D-E-A-D. I can't even imagine.

And when I try to think what it would be like to be him, I really don't think he does anything on purpose to be mean. Not even what he did to me. It's just that he's in a rage all the time.

And he has a right to be. What happened to him is so unfair. It says in the paper that his parents are calling it murder. I don't know if that's true, I don't know if somebody is going to get charged with murder, but the District Attorney is asking anybody who knows anything about how that cable got there to come forward.

No wonder Daddy is drinking.

I know I'm not going to be able to sleep tonight.

Tuesday morning.

I'm not getting up. I can't face school. I can't face anything.

I've got to get up. I've got to go to the bathroom. Life's not fair. If I'm supposed to sleep eight hours, why've I got a seven-hour bladder?

Dusty joked to herself to try to feel better. It

didn't work. She had barely slept at all, and when she had dozed, her dreams had been full of shouting and black wings and the hammering of angry hooves. Lying and staring up into another day, she felt a stony sense of wrongness sitting like a gargoyle on her chest.

Get up, Destiny.

She pulled her knees to her chest to try to stretch her back, then got herself moving. Her back hurt as she hobbled to the bathroom, but what else was new? It was the same as it had been for a while and was always going to be. She brushed her teeth, ran a soggy washcloth over her face, looked for her pain pills . . . Had she left them in the kitchen again? Must have. Two-footing the steps like an old person, hanging on to the railing, she struggled down the stairs to find them.

Her father was sitting at the kitchen table, still in his rumpled suit, pale and stubbly, looking worse than she felt. He was drinking something from a stoneware mug. "Dusty," he said hoarsely, "call the office, wouldja, tell them I won't be in. Tell them I've got the bug."

Dusty stalled by reaching for her pills and dispensing herself a glass of water from the gizmo in the refrigerator door. She stared at her father as she dosed herself. "What's in the cup?" She did not smell coffee.

"Just make the damn call."

She did: "Yeah . . . uh-huh . . . I guess he's got what's going around." She knew by the coy tone in her father's secretary's voice that the woman knew she was lying. Dusty hoped she thought he was just calling in sick to avoid going out in public. She hoped nobody knew yet that he was drinking again, hung over.

I've got to stop doing this. It was the same thing she had done when her father had first started drinking—protecting him, defending him, making excuses for him, lying to cover up for him—and she knew it was no good. But there she was, doing it anyway.

She hung up the phone and turned to face him. "Okay," she said, "tell me."

Bleary-eyed, he blinked up at her.

"The cable across the woods trail," she said, trying to keep her voice quiet and steady. She didn't want it to sound like she was accusing him.

But she might as well have pointed her finger at him. His face flushed high-blood-pressure red, and he lunged up, bumping the table and splashing his drink across the cloth. "Nobody can prove a thing!" He shouted so hard, his voice cracked. "Anyway, it's my land. That boy was trespassing!"

This was true, Dusty knew. Skye had no right to be on somebody else's land, and the landowner had every right to try to keep him off. To order him off at gunpoint, even. *Trespassing:* the word was legal, but—but it didn't feel right. Back when Mom was alive, kids were welcome on Grove land, as welcome as the butterflies that flitted across the meadow. What Dad was saying felt wrong to Dusty. Its stony weight pressed so hard and hurtfully on her chest that she could not speak.

Her father kept right on shouting. "Anybody could have put that thing there. They can't charge me with a damn thing, and they know it, and they aren't about to."

This also had some truth to it. There was something called reasonable doubt, or shadow of a doubt, or whatever. Also—Dusty didn't like this part much—Daddy knew who he was: Abel Grove, the man providing paychecks for half the people in Grovesburg. Even the press didn't want to get in his face. And the police and district attorney would be very careful. They wouldn't charge Abel Grove with any crime unless they were very, very sure of their case.

Dusty whispered, "Skye's dead."

And instead of accepting any sort of responsibility, moral, legal, or whatever, there stood Daddy in a drunken rage. Even sober, Daddy could never handle being in the wrong. When Mom was around, she used to let him hand her the blame for anything he shouldn't have done or forgot to do, like returning a phone call. Little things, mostly.

This was no little thing. It was an enormity—so huge, almost incomprehensible, that Dusty said it again. "Skye's *dead*."

Still yelling, her father probably didn't hear her. He probably heard only himself. "There's a sign right at the trail head, says *Keep out!*" Red-faced, red-eyed, he loomed toward her, leaning on the table. She stepped back. "Nobody had any business being in those woods. Nobody had any business going on that trail. If he went back there, well, it's his own fault."

"It's the ugliest thing I ever heard of," Dusty said, loud enough to make sure he heard her. Her voice shook. She ran for her room, slammed the door behind her and locked it.

He didn't follow her. He stayed downstairs.

He hadn't told her a thing about the cable across the woods trail. But he didn't have to. Dusty knew who had put it there.

"No," she whispered. No, she would not think it. No, it could not be true. The police couldn't prove anything. They could not take her father away. If they took him away, she would have nothing, nobody. She had to keep him. She had to protect him. He would stop drinking again when he knew it was going to be okay. And Skye could just ride Tazz somewhere far, far away and stay there. Skye could just stay away from her father.

Dusty hid in her room until early afternoon. The phone rang several times, probably the school calling to find out where she was. Or maybe reporters. Dusty did not know, because she did not venture out to answer it. No one answered it. Each time after five rings the answering machine picked up and took the calls.

Around one o'clock, Dusty got hungry, opened her door softly and padded downstairs, her sneakers nearly soundless on the carpeting. She found her father passed out again in almost the same place as before. She left him there, went to the kitchen, and made herself a peanut-butter-and-strawberry-jam sandwich and ate it. She did not listen to the messages on the answering machine.

Around two o'clock she saw the police car coming down the driveway and walked outside, locking the door behind her.

"Miss?" one of the cops called to her. There were two of them.

She stood still and waited. The cop on the passenger side got out of the car. He was a young cop. Nice looking.

"Miss, uh, Destiny Grove?"

She nodded.

"Is your father home?"

She shook her head.

"You sure?" The cop was hinting that it would be okay for her to change her mind. "His office says he didn't go in today."

"I don't know where he is, then." She took a couple of steps toward the barn, as if she had been going to check on the horses. It was about time somebody checked on them anyway.

"You mind if we have a look around?"

She felt her heart pounding but hoped she looked bored and annoyed. "Aren't you supposed to have a warrant or something?"

The cop behind the wheel, older, not cute, poked his head out of his window and snapped, "Aren't you supposed to be in school?"

"I have a back injury. It's acting up today."

"We really need to talk with your father," the young cop said.

"I'm phoning the school," the older cop said, reaching down toward his dashboard. "See whether you're excused."

"It's about the incident this past Friday." The young cop tilted his head toward the wooded ridge where the trail ran. "You heard about that?"

"Of course I heard."

"Did you know the Ryder boy?"

She shook her head, realizing with a sudden pang that she wished she had known Skye when he was alive.

"Do you know who strung that cable there?"

"No."

"Whoever strung it that way," the older cop barked out of the cruiser window, "is liable for criminal misdemeanor at the very least, and maybe manslaughter, which carries a sentence of two to five years."

Dusty purposely unfocused her eyes in order to look bored silly, then turned toward him. "Did you call the school?"

"Huh?"

"You were going to call the school to see whether my father phoned my excuse in."

He blinked. She was yanking his chain, knowing darn well he had never called. Cops had better things to do than chase truants, or considered that they did. He was just trying to scare her and she knew it and he didn't like her for knowing it. "You know where your father is?" he snapped.

"If he isn't at his office, how would I?"

The cop puffed his cheeks in exasperation.

"Just tell him to contact us, would you, miss?" the other one said. Without waiting for an answer he got back in the cruiser, which made a pretty impressive roar as it drove a loop around Dusty and headed back up the driveway. She stood there a minute longer, then continued toward the barn in case they might be parked along the road, watching.

She needed to cry, but the need was like a lump of ice in her chest. She couldn't let it melt. Cold willpower was the only thing holding her together. If she let down her guard even for a minute, they would come and take her father away and stick her in an orphanage or something. A mental institution if she let them know that she was seeing spirits, that she was cracked in the head like her mother.

In the barn, she paused by the wall where Tazz's bridle hung, and his halter and blanket. She laid her head against the blanket and closed her eyes, whiffing Tazz's warm, fox-red smell still on the cloth, trying to pretend he was there. But it did not help as much as she would have liked. She knew he was gone.

She took a carrot and a scoop of grain to the little pony in the paddock. Kneeling in the dirt, she watched him eat. "Pinocchio," she whispered. "Pinoke." He was a shaggy little thing, all chin whiskers at this time of year, looking gravely back at her. Shedding. He needed to be groomed. Everybody needed something.

"Pinoke, sweetie, what am I gonna do?" Just

whispering the words made her eyes sting. *Damn, no crying.* "Oh, help," Dusty muttered, swallowing at the clotted feeling in her throat. Trying to lighten up, trying to make herself feel better, she told Pinocchio gravely, "Pinoke, I am in deep doggy doo-doo. I need a break. I need an option. I need a winning lottery ticket."

Pinocchio gave her a bored look.

"Your nose is growing," she told him, because it was fun to watch him not be insulted. She'd been telling Pinoke for years that his nose was growing, and he didn't care.

It was Mama who had given Pinocchio his name, because little-girl Dusty had seen the pony's petite muzzle as ever so long.

Mama. Oh, God. Dusty had to close her stinging eyes. She heard the pony snort in satisfaction as he finished eating, felt his soft muzzle against her shoulder. Still trying to joke, she whispered, "Pinoke, I need . . . I need my mommy."

And for just a moment she felt an odd waft of peace.

Chapter Five

That night, sleeping on her straw-bale bed in the barn, she dreamed of her mother.

She was sleeping in the barn because she liked it out there. It felt cleaner there than in the house, where Daddy lay drunk with his AA buddy baby-sitting him. Outside, the night air was fresh and cool, the night sky, so deep. The stars, so white— angel eyes, Mom used to call them. Dusty had made her bed with her head almost outside the big barn door so that she could sleep amid stars, velvety sky, a chalky hoof-paring of crescent moon, shadowy pasture and indigo hills.

In the dream, Mom was a dead person, like Skye

yet not like Skye. Always Skye seemed vivid, supercharged, made of shadows and electricity, like a thunderhead filled with heat lightning. But Mom— Julia was her name, beautiful name, Julia Grove— Julia/Mom was a gauzy presence, a breeze caught in white organza, the fragrance of lilacs in the rain. Dusty knew Skye to be beautiful, but he was a crayon drawing compared to Mother in the dream. Her eyes were purple witching glasses. Yet they were fireflies. Yet they were her eyes. Her voice was a wren singing. Yet it was green corn rustling. Yet Mom.

Mom, as warm as fresh-baked bread, giving her the same old loopy smile. "Sweetie," Mom said as if continuing a conversation they had started long before, "you have no idea. Aaak, the responsibility."

Gazing into her mother's starwhisper face, Dusty wanted to say something, but she couldn't. She was asleep.

"Keeping the logs," Mom prattled on, "and reporting to the arch-supervisor, and trying to guide without interfering, and it's not just Skye, either, it's all those other struggling souls."

In her dream, Dusty floated face to face with her mother, elbows on the air, as if they were sitting at the kitchen table—in the air? Her mother was talking to her as she used to converse with spirits.

Were there wings? If Mom had wings, they were made of moonfire. Dusty wanted to look for her own wings, but she did not want to take her eyes from her mother's face.

"Although I must say I worry about Skye the most," Mom confided. Mom's voice was the distant chiming of spring peepers. Wind in trees on the far hills. A whippoorwill calling. "The afterlife is so terribly permanent," she said. "I know you're having problems, Dusty, but even if your father goes to jail, it'll be just for two years, five years. That's an eyeblink. Just a wink in eternity. Time will pass and you will be fine. But Skye . . . you have to understand, sweetie, he could be doomed for all time."

It seemed to Dusty in her dream that the kitchen was kind of a mess, as always, even though it was made of air and starlight, but from somewhere there were flowers in Mom's hands, moonflowers to be arranged in the crystal vase of night.

"He needs to transcend, he needs to fly away to eternity," her mother was saying as she sorted the flowers. "But anger is holding him back. He's in soul peril. He could be trapped in his rage forever."

Forever is a very long time, Dusty wanted to joke, but Mom handed her a flower the color of a star. "You're so much like your father," she said, and

Dusty heard a quirk of tenderness in the words, a midnight echo of the way Mama had loved Daddy when she was alive.

I am? Dusty thought, and she wanted to ask what Mom meant, but she couldn't. She could only breathe in the fragrance of her flower; it smelled like a rainbow. She was asleep.

Whatever Mama meant, it was all right. Mama had loved Daddy.

Mom was the scent of white clover, lace curtains drying on the line, wild hyacinths. Her gauzy manifestation dislimned into starlight. But her voice grew closer, warmer. "Sleep well, darling."

Dusty slept well. When she awoke at dawn, Pinocchio stood in the barn, nodding over her, his grass-scented breath warm on her face.

Mom, Dusty thought, feeling that warmth. *What a good dream.*

What a goofy dream. Just a dream. Struggling to sit up, her back aching, she forgot all about it within a few moments; it was gone like wisps of morning mist in the sunlight. But she was left with a feeling of strength—and a sense of urgency.

At first she could not think what was so terribly important. But then she knew. To the marrow of her mortal bones she knew.

Skye.

Skye was in soul peril. Danger so deep she could barely comprehend.

DAILY SOULOG ANNO DOMINI 1998, 4TH MOON, 22ND DAY
Subject Skye Ryder, all too adolescent, continuing in ghost phase. Best hope at this point lies in Destiny Grove, equally adolescent, but visionary and therefore wiser. Providentially, Destiny has chosen to dream about me, enabling me to visit her and speak to her about Skye. Visit may indirectly help him, yet would not be considered actual intervention were the question to arise. Conscience nags: Is this line of thinking specious, too much like the rationalizations of my poor, hurting, erstwhile husband? He told himself that he just meant to scare, not really hurt anyone; I am telling myself that I am just talking with my daughter, not really meddling. Is my thinking as muddled as his was? Perhaps. But now conscience comforts: My heart is filled with concern. Not with fear and spleen, like Abel's. Even specious thoughts cannot send one too far wrong when there is a caring heart. It will be all right; I think my actions are not too terribly misguided. Maintaining discreet vigilance,

J. G., Sector Supervisor

In the house, Dusty found the man from Alcoholics Anonymous resting in an armchair but her father nowhere in sight. "He's sleeping," the AA man reported. He was a coveralled, tobacco-chewing garage mechanic, could not have been more different from Daddy except that they were both drunks. Well, this guy was a recovering alcoholic and Daddy had turned back into a drunk. There was a difference. "He's sleeping in his bed for a change. When he gets up, he doesn't know it yet but he's going to get showered and shaved and get his butt to work. You got someplace you can lay low?"

"I'll go to school."

She took the bus, then once she got to school she couldn't concentrate. All day she did nothing but think of Skye and track down kids who had known him. Boys who had ridden bikes with him, mostly. Not that many kids. She found out that Skye had a younger brother her age, but he was taking a week off school. Just as well; she would not have wanted to hurt him with her questions. She spent the day passing notes in class, talking with kids in the echoing cafeteria at lunch. Talking about Skye.

Except when she was interrupted by Katelyn. "How's your father?" Katelyn asked, yelling to be heard above the noise.

Dusty shrugged. She didn't want to talk about her father. Her father had been sober for a year and now he was drinking again and there didn't seem to be anything she could count on or anything she could do about him.

"Aren't you going to eat?" Katelyn wanted her to sit with her as usual.

"No."

"God's sake, at least sit down and have a cheese cracker."

"No, thanks."

Katelyn scowled and tapped her purple plastic fingernails against the table. "What's it with you and that dead kid, anyway?"

"I just want to find out what he was like." Dusty wanted to know, and somehow it made her feel better to talk about him.

"You think your father did it," Katelyn said, just loud enough so that Dusty could hear. "You think he did it, don't you?"

Dusty wanted to hit her. Hard. But her back hurt, and Skye was dead, and how would hitting help anything? Dusty turned away, biting her lip, and went to talk with a boy she barely knew about Skye.

Skye was nice, he said. That was what everyone said. Skye had been a nice kid who lived over the hill from the Nisleys. Did crazy things sometimes, like ride his dirt bike over a railroad trestle. Liked to go fast. Liked animals and nature. Liked to get out in the woods and ride.

When Dusty got home that afternoon, her father's Bronco was parked in the driveway but the house was empty. A scrawled note left under the salt shaker on the kitchen table told her that Steve (the AA guy) had dropped her father off at his office and would pick him up and bring him home.

Dusty wandered down to the fence and stood for a long time just looking at the horses. She thought of Katelyn, Ms. Purple Plastic Fingernails, then pushed the thought away. Whether to forgive Katelyn for what she had said was the least of her worries. She tried to give herself a break for a minute, tried not to think of anything at all, shifting from foot to foot to try to ease her aching back. She wanted to go lie down.

It kind of seemed as if she had spent the past couple of years lying down.

In the pasture there were two chestnut mares, mother and daughter. There was old Pinocchio. There was a seal-brown Appaloosa without any spots. The mares had been for pleasure riding, the Appaloosa had been Mom's jumper. All were just expensive lawn ornaments now, and if the grass got thin Daddy threw them some hay. The vet came twice a year. Other than that, nobody bothered with them much.

But Tazz . . . Razzle My Tazz had been different. Where was he now?

Where was Skye?

She had told him to go away. She had been afraid of him. What would he do if he found out it was . . . it was her father who had killed him? Which it was. No use pretending it wasn't.

Funny, she felt more worried about Skye than she did about her father.

She couldn't go lie down. She had to do something.

But what?

"What am I supposed to do?" she said softly to Pinocchio. "I've got to help somehow. Whatever happens to Skye, it's forever."

The old pony lifted his shaggy little head and looked back at her. His eyes were midnight deep, indigo witching glasses.

Dusty said, "I told him to go away. I guess I ought to go find him."

Pinocchio's gaze told her nothing, yet everything. She turned and walked back to the house as quickly as she could. She grabbed the keys from her father's dresser and headed out.

*   *   *

She took the Bronco.

Driving without a license. Underage. Automobile theft, grand larceny, maybe.

I'm as crazy as Skye was.

As crazy as my mother.

It felt good.

And it wasn't hard. Driving on the country roads wasn't that different from driving around the farm. Barely any traffic. And she didn't have far to go. Within five minutes she had navigated a rutted gravel road and parked in front of the red metal gate with its nasty KEEP OUT sign. Leaving the car, she walked into the woods.

"Skye?"

No answer.

Because her errand was so strange, the familiar trail seemed strange. And something had changed. The yellow police tape was gone from around the crime scene. It was just another patch of woods now.

"Skye? Tazz?"

They weren't there.

They really weren't there. *I'd know it if they were here. I'd feel it even if I couldn't see it.*

The woods stood sunny and placid all around. Dusty turned and walked back to the car.

Okay. She knew Skye considered himself a ghost. *Where else would he be hanging around?*

His family? His home?

On the other side of the hill from Nisley's, kids had said. Dusty started the Bronco and bumped her way out to the hard road, gritting her teeth against the pain in her back. She drove slowly, looking for a mailbox that said Ryder.

Even though they lived just over the hills, less than a mile away from her house, the road wound around for three or four miles before she found the Ryders' place. There it was. She turned in at the unpaved lane without giving herself time to think. If she thought about it, she knew, what she was doing would scare her so badly she would head home to her room and lock the door and never come out again. Yet it did not feel wrong. It felt crazy and deeply right.

Why? She could tell within a moment that Skye wasn't there.

It was one of those prefab houses set down on a concrete-block foundation plopped onto a scalped piece of former cow pasture, dirt still raw around it, no grass, no trees, no history or memories. Not the kind of place a ghost would haunt. Skye probably hadn't lived here more than a few months before he died.

On the stark new patio a man, a woman, and three boys sat staring at her.

Dusty realized that she had turned off the

Bronco and was just sitting in it. She also realized that any sensible person would turn it back on and roar out of there. Instead, she opened her door and heaved herself upright. It was hard to stand up.

"You lost, honey?" the woman called. Skye's mother. She had his dark hair and shadowy eyes. A sweet tone in her voice. Probably a sweet smile, though Dusty could see that right now she could not smile; she had the haggard look of someone who was just hanging on.

Dusty had some idea how she felt. She remembered how it had felt after her mother died.

The three boys, Skye's brothers, all looked like him, too. Or like subdued, earthen versions of the spirit Dusty knew. The father was a sandy-haired man who looked at first as if he didn't fit in until Dusty saw his chiseled chin and the anger in his eyes.

"Can we help you?" the mother asked.

"Maybe," Dusty said, limping toward them. "Well, no." And she wasn't sure whether she could help them, either.

"You looking for somebody?"

She nodded. But she couldn't just say the name of the person she was looking for. It would hurt them. Instead she said, "Please don't get mad at me. I don't mean to bother you. Please don't think I'm some kind of nut."

Now the father was scowling at her. His scowl was just like Skye's.

She said, "They thought my mother was kind of nutty. She saw spirits. Now it's happening to me, too."

Maybe she was nuts, talking with these people. But she couldn't just go away. The urgent heartbeat in her chest would not let her.

The father said, "You're that Grove girl."

She nodded to him. She said, "I've seen Skye."

Chapter Six

The father's face flushed angrily. He sat up straight to tell her she'd better leave. But as he drew his breath and opened his mouth the mother's voice came flying like a dove. "Where? How? Tell me!" Each word quivered like a swallow's wings. "Did he talk to you? What did he say?"

Dusty turned to see the woman stretching shaky hands toward her, face lifted toward her, leaning forward in her chair so far it looked as if she would fall. Dusty grabbed her trembling hands. "Shhh, Mrs. Ryder. Yes, he talked to me. Shhh, I'll tell you everything."

*   *   *

"Then—he's a troubled soul."

Dusty nodded.

"He hasn't found peace."

"No. Not yet." It was dusk, Dusty realized. She had been talking with the Ryders for hours. At some time she had sat down on the concrete by Skye's mother's feet. The boys had crowded their chairs around, listening—they were handsome, silent, with eyes that spoke for them; had he been that way? Mr. Ryder had brought her water in a tall glass with ice cubes. He sat listening, too, leaning back with his arms folded across his chest.

"He needs to be at peace," Skye's mother said softly. "How can he find it? What can we do?"

Dusty sighed. She didn't have an answer.

Mr. Ryder spoke up for the first time, his voice quiet but harsh. "Dusty. Who put that cable across the trail?"

She looked down. "I don't know."

"I think you do know."

Turning as if every movement were an effort, his wife told him, "Hush."

"I can't hush. Our son is dead."

"Have mercy," Mrs. Ryder said, her voice muted. Both of them spoke so softly that Dusty did not feel they were quarreling. She sensed that they craved comfort, but in such different ways that they could not console each other.

"Mercy? No one had mercy on Skye."

"Dusty can't help that."

"I think she can help."

"How? She didn't do it."

"Maybe not, but talk about troubled souls, look at her! She knows who did."

There was a breath of silence. Then, gently enough, Mr. Ryder said, "Dusty."

She managed to raise her head and meet his gaze.

He said, "Look, I believe you really do want peace for Skye. But the way I figure, there can't be peace till there's justice."

Dusty mumbled, "I really don't know anything." That was the truth. She knew nothing for sure. But she was thinking of her father, and her heart hurt.

"But you really have been seeing Skye's spirit?"

"Yes!"

"Don't you figure there's a reason for that?"

Staring at the patio floor again, Dusty felt Skye's mother's hand settle like a butterfly on her hair. "Honey," she told her husband, answering for Dusty, "I figure, yes, there is a reason for that."

Silence.

Something seemed settled, but Dusty was not sure how or what. Thinking of her father, she felt a pang that echoed the grief around her. "I'd better get home," she said, her voice faltering. She started struggling to her feet.

Skye's father stood up, reached down, and lifted her to her feet as if she were a little kid. He was strong. "I should have given you my chair," he grumbled. "You sitting on that hard concrete, what the heck was I thinking of? I'm getting senile."

The boys actually smiled, almost laughed. Their names were Canyon, Craig, Leigh. Dusty wasn't clear yet about which ones were older and which ones were younger or how Skye had fit in.

Skye. They had to miss him so much. "I'm sorry," she said to all of them.

"Don't be sorry." It was Mr. Ryder. "I hope you'll come back. I don't know what to think of all this spirit stuff, but—"

"Tell us if you see him again." It was one of the boys, low-voiced Canyon.

"At least he has the horse," Mrs. Ryder said. "That's really something. I bet he loves that horse. Now I'll have a picture in my mind when I try to sleep tonight." She smiled, and yes, she did have the sweetest smile in the county. "Instead of picturing him in that grave, I'll think of him riding that horse. Out there under the stars."

*   *   *

When Dusty got home, her father was there alone, and he was not drinking. He was not doing anything but slouching in an armchair and staring at the living room wall.

"Hi," Dusty said.

His eyes barely flickered to glance at her before they fixed on the wall again. "Where you been?"

"Out driving around."

Dusty stood there, waiting, almost hoping. The kind of father he used to be, he should want to know a lot more about where she had been for four hours without leaving a note, and he should have a lot more to say about her driving illegally to get there. But he did not react to what she had said at all. He barely seemed to hear her.

She sat down across from him, in front of his patch of wall. "Did you have something to eat?"

His eyes focused on her slowly.

"Are you hungry?" she tried again. *She* was hungry. When she was a kid—heck, she was still a kid; somebody ought to feed her. Somebody ought to ask about her, how her day had been, and offer her hot food. Roast chicken. Pot pie. Soup. . . .

Her father shook his head. Stared some more.

Dusty asked, "Are you all right?"

It took him a moment to come back to her. "What?"

"I asked, are you all right?"

His lips pressed together. "Just let me alone."

She got up and headed to the kitchen to find herself something to eat.

There wasn't even a can of tuna. Obviously Daddy hadn't gone grocery shopping lately. *Where's that maid?* Dusty joked sourly to herself as she put together an unsatisfactory meal of ketchup sandwiches on toasted stale bread. *What's the use of that lazy maid?* To eat, she sat down where she couldn't see her father sitting in the living room and staring.

I wonder what's going on in his head.

But she found she didn't have a clue. She didn't know him well enough. He didn't talk to her, or not that way. He had all the usual good, fatherly feelings for her, she could tell, but he would never say so. He didn't like to talk about feelings. Didn't want to talk about Mom, either. He worked hard, came home, was tired, went back to work the next day. She barely understood what he did there. On weekends he watched sports, mowed grass, read the *Wall Street Journal*. He talked about baseball or complained about government and the high prices of everything. When was the last time she had really talked with her father? Had she ever?

They're gonna take him away and stick me in a Home For Hapless Children.

The thought was an attempt at a joke, but it turned her cold to the core. Ever since Mom had died, Dusty had been afraid that she would be left with no one.

It was not a fear she had ever spoken to her father.

Why hadn't she tried harder to talk to him? Was she really kind of like him? Somebody was saying she was like him; who had said that? She couldn't remember.

There he sat, yet . . .

Heck, I might as well be an orphan.

Dusty stood up, leaving her unfinished "dinner" on the table, and fled to her room. But closing her door couldn't shut the problems out. Like ghosts, problems traveled through doors. Went wherever they wanted. Haunting her.

Dusty looked at her homework with no more comprehension than her father had shown when he had looked at her. Then she turned off her light and stood at her window. Downstairs, her father was staring at a wall. Upstairs, she was staring into the night.

As her eyes adjusted to the darkness, she began to see colors. Green-black sheen of the pond in the pasture bottom. Teal velvet pasture hills. Deep indigo infinity between the stars. The window glass became annoying, a barrier between her and the night.

Skye was out there. Somewhere.

At the thought of him, Dusty felt her chest swell with wanting. Needing. She needed to see him. She needed to look upon his shining shoulders, his beautiful, fiery face and try to gentle him with her voice, like trying to gentle a proud colt. To see him, talk with him, tell him that his mother loved him, his father, his brothers, they all missed him and loved him. Tell him—

Whoa.

It was mainly that he was in danger, wasn't it? Skye was in terrible peril. Not sure how she could help, but . . .

"Have to find him," Dusty muttered, and she headed downstairs and out, grabbing her ketchup sandwich on the way, not even turning to see whether her father noticed as she left.

The Bronco, too, would have been a barrier between her and the night. Cars needed to stay on roads. Dusty headed out on foot, cross-country, without a flashlight. It was a good feeling. Back when she had still been able to ride horses, sometimes she had ridden out at night, no flashlight—light would have gotten in the way—and she remembered the feeling, how she had become part of the horse and the horse had become part of the night. She tried to feel that sure, that powerful, as she strode down the first long pasture slope and past the pond.

Her mind felt oddly sure. Her heart felt sure. But her body felt not sure at all. Her back hurt, and the pain weakened her. With every step on the uneven ground her back hurt more. When her foot came down on an unseen rock or in an unseen hollow, her back hurt atrociously.

"Damn. I can't. . . ." Panting with pain, she had to stand still. Couldn't go any farther. No duh; why had her fool head started thinking she could do the things she used to do? Good grief, it had been how long since the accident? Time enough to know better. She knew she couldn't go hiking around—

But I have to find Skye!

Where was he?

He should be haunting his death site. But he had not been there that afternoon. So he could be anywhere.

Dusty looked around at dark hills, a freckle drift of stars, a silver wisp of moon. Her breathing quieted. She listened to the rippling of water in the pond, the breeze in the evergreens. She sighed, and caught the faint fragrance of bluebells.

Something made her think of her mother. For

just a whisper of an instant it was as if she could see Mom sitting at a kitchen table in the night sky, cradling flowers as white as moonlight in a crystal amethyst vase, talking with spirits.

How did Mom do that? How did she find her angels; how did she know they were there?

Standing amid starlit night, Dusty closed her eyes. "Mom," she whispered, meaning *Let me be more like her.*

The thought spooked her a little, because to be like Mom was to be, well, different. According to most people, crazy.

"So what," Dusty muttered. It was a crazy world.

She took a deep breath and let it out slowly, then stood as still as the night, just—just being there. Hearkening. Waiting for something, she wasn't sure what. Trying to be brave. Trying to feel a presence in the night.

"Skye?" she whispered. "Where are you?"

Fear knifed into her like a lightning bolt, jolting her eyes open. *Danger.*

Terrible peril.

But not so much for her as for him. Skye. Somewhere Skye was in serious trouble.

Dusty sensed this in a wordless moment, not so much understanding as feeling—she had to help, she had to help, she had to find him. "Oh," she

whispered, and then she stamped her foot and—
she wanted to yell, but it came out a whimper
because everything hurt. "Oh. Skye, you idiot,
where *are* you?"

A white shadow moved. Dusty jumped, then
stared, then trusted other senses more, hearing the
sound of small hooves, smelling a warm grassy
odor. She smiled as Pinocchio trotted up to her like
a big dog.

"Pinoke." She reached out to touch his shaggy
back. Without pausing, he trotted around her as if
she were a goal post, swiveling her.

"Pinoke?" she whispered. "You know?" But
duh, of course he knew. Horses saw spirits all
the time.

Pinocchio slowed just a little to head back
downhill.

Dusty set her teeth, hung on to his furry back,
and followed.

It was all she could do to keep up with him. She
jarred along at her fastest walk, panting more with
pain than with exertion. God, she hated this, she
hated not being able to run and ride and do things,
she hated feeling crippled. She hated her father
when he was drunk; she hated what his drunk
driving had done to her.

They were heading . . . back toward the house?

"Pin-oc-chi-o," Dusty panted, "what—"

The she saw. No thunder sounded, and no thunder of hoofbeats, either, but there might as well have been thunder and lightning. At a hard, headlong, eerily silent gallop, Tazz swept like a red storm out of the forest, over the fence with no more effort than wind, down the pasture.

Red? Yes, Dusty could see him red in the night, aglow like a horse made of fire. She could see Skye riding the way she used to ride, like a lick of white fire on the big horse's back.

No, not like her. Dusty knew that she herself had never been so beautiful, or so incandescent with rage.

She ran toward Skye, or tried to run.

It occurred to her that she ought to be afraid. Any sane person would be afraid. But there was no time, she had to concentrate on fighting her pain—every step felt as though it was going to kill her—and since when had she been sane anyway?

"Skye!" she cried.

If he heard her he gave no sign of it. He was ahead of her, galloping toward the house. She would never reach him in time.

"Skye! Your mother wants me to tell you—"

Tazz skidded, wheeled, reared. Spectral hooves struck at the air above Dusty's head. Skye's fierce face glared down at her. "*What?*" he shouted. "*What* did you say?"

As if facing an angry, frightened colt, Dusty stood still and kept her voice level and low. "I was talking with your family—"

Tazz's forehooves plummeted to the ground beside her. No thud, just a weird silence as the horse stood inches from her. She could see his flared nostrils, but she could not hear his breathing. His eyes were absences in his red, glowing head. It was Tazz, her own beloved Tazz, yet she did not dare to touch him.

She said very quietly to Skye, "They miss you a lot. Your father, your mother, your brothers. I went to see them—"

"You—you scum! Stay away from them! Don't you go near them!"

She had known that he was furiously angry, but not that he was angry at her. What had changed? Surprise made her stand there with nothing sensible to say. "But they're worried about you," she whispered.

"You don't deserve to know them. Traitor."

"I—"

"You let me think you were my friend! When your father is the one who killed me!"

Oh.

Somehow he had found out, or figured it out. He felt betrayed. Dusty stood aching, with no answer for him, because what he had said was all too likely true. Even though she'd had nothing to do with what had happened, a wordless guilt made her silent.

"He is a murderer. And it looks like he is going to get away with it in this world. But I know a world where he will not get away with it." Skye reached out to tug on Tazz's black-fire mane and turn him away from her.

She could barely believe what she was hearing.

Yet—yet she did believe. "You're going to—you're going to kill him?"

"Yes," he said curtly over his shoulder. "With one touch of a fingertip. I have that power."

She knew he did. She had already seen and felt his power.

In a lightning flash of intuition as deep as sky, as deep as her mother's eyes, Destiny comprehended the full meaning of soul peril, and she felt dread settle upon her like a mantle the size of the night and far darker. *Oh, Skye.* If he used the power to kill, he would no longer have the power to heal—not others, not himself. He would be dead, soul dead, for eternity, more dead than her father would be.

And already he was riding away.

Shaken as if she had been struck, trembling, Dusty did not know how to make him see how wrong his hatred was. And how deadly. How final.

She tried. "You want to be a murderer, too?" she shouted after him as fiercely as he had shouted at her.

"As if I care, traitor girl?" His voice floated back to her as he cantered away.

Chapter Seven

On Tazz, Skye shot across the pasture like a comet in the night. Dusty ran after him, jarring her back so badly that tears ran; she sobbed with each step—but it was no use. Skye was going to reach the house before she could hobble past the pond.

On—my—horse.

Suddenly she was furious. She yelled, "Tazz!"

Ten years had to count for something. When Tazz was a fuzzy brown baby and she was not much more than a fuzzy baby herself, she had napped in the straw with him, she had pillowed her head on his softly breathing side. When Tazz was a little older, she had slipped his first soft halter on him. When he was a yearling, she had put the rubber bit in his mouth and walked behind him with the long reins. She had saddle trained him so gently that he had never been frightened, not once. And after that they had always been together. Whole days of riding. Camping trips in the mountains, racing the deer.

"Ta-azz!"

She saw him hesitate, then surge forward again.

Her anger was gone, but all the memories were in her voice as she cried out, "Razzle My *Tazz!*"

He whinnied, and the weird red-fire light in him flickered out. Still galloping fast and proudly, he swung in a wide circle, speeding back toward her, flashing like crystal in the night, with a ghostly sheen. Even though Skye's hands were tugging his mane and Skye's heels were thumping his sides, Tazz slid to a cow-pony stop in front of her, his eyes shining like dark moons. She put a hand on his forehead, and he arched his neck so that she could rub the itchy place between his ears.

"You—you total traitor!" Skye could scarcely speak, he was so furious. "You gave him to me!"

She had no intention of taking Tazz away from him, Tazz glimmering like a ghost, Tazz belonging so obviously to an afterworld now. But let Skye think what he liked, the idiot. Dusty shot back at him, "And what have you given me?"

"I healed you!"

"For five minutes once. Then you took it away. Just like that."

On Tazz's back, he sat still. His beautiful face had gone intently still. He whispered, "I did?"

"You mean to tell me you haven't *noticed*?"

"I . . . I've been so mad—" But then his lips closed into a hard line. "Why should I care?" he said between his teeth. "You're his daughter."

He pulled back on Tazz's mane, trying to wheel away. But Dusty kept her hand on Tazz's head, and Tazz stayed where he was.

"What do you want?" Skye yelled at her. "You want your horse back?" He made it sound like a threat.

Not if it meant having Tazz lame or dead, no. She shook her head.

"What, then?"

She knew better than to say it to him, but she wanted what his mother wanted; she wanted him to be at peace. And . . . maybe peace did require justice.

She tilted her head back to look straight at him up on the tall horse, to meet his smoldering gaze. She said, "Give me a little time to talk with my father."

When she limped into the house, her father was still sitting in the same place, staring at the same wall.

She stood in the doorway. "Dad?"

He did not look at her. He had not looked at her when she came in.

"*Daddy*. Listen to me. They're coming to get you."

For a moment nothing happened, and then his head moved. His eyes, focused on her, were like the eyes of a suffering animal. Pain, fear. Not much else there.

She asked him, "Did you do it? Did you put that cable there?"

Now there was a flash of anger. He moved his mouth, spoke. "You're my daughter." His voice was scratchy, as if he was having trouble using it. "Whose side are you on?"

His daughter—but what did she feel for him? She couldn't tell whether she loved him or she was stuck with him. "You've been drinking," she said. "I ate ketchup sandwiches for supper."

"So?"

"So maybe it would be better if you went to jail! At least you wouldn't get drunk there. And if you did—" She couldn't say it, the K-word: *kill*. She felt sure he hadn't meant to kill anyone. This was her father; she knew him. This was the daddy who had read her horsie books when she was little. And then when she was a bit older, set her on her first pony. Gave her a leg up at her first big show. Fixed her tack-box latch, hitched the horse trailer, made a wooden sign, RAZZLE MY TAZZ, for the stall door. She knew that he was kind and she also knew that he tripped over his own ego a lot of the time, he could be stupid that way. "If you are the one . . . who put that cable there—"

"Nobody can prove anything!"

"Dad, I don't care! If you did it, then . . ." What in God's name was she going to say to him to make him understand that he had worse things than jail to fear? That she *was* on his side? That she was trying to save him? "If you did it, you have to face up to it."

He didn't seem to hear her at all. He wasn't looking at her. "Nobody can prove that I personally did a thing!" It was as though he was chanting his mantra. "Nobody can prove that I did it."

Something chilled Dusty's spine, and she listened to the night. She heard nothing. No door opened and closed. But no door had to. She felt an incorporeal breath in the air. A presence.

She said to her father, "Don't tell it to me. Tell it to him." She turned.

Skye was there. Right behind her.

Skye stood in the dark kitchen, now lighted by his white-hot righteous rage. Skye stood no taller than any ordinary person, yet he seemed vast. He was just a sixteen-year-old boy who had been killed, a kid whose photo had been in the paper, a kid who would mostly be forgotten by the time the newspaper went into the garbage—yet he was the universe, all the dying, all the crying. He was everyone who had ever died young.

With no sound of footsteps, he walked past Dusty, toward her father. He shone as hard as porcelain. Halfway between Dusty and her father, he stopped and stood like a knife made of white fire. Like embodied lightning.

Dusty's father stumbled up from his armchair with a hoarse shout and backed away.

"He sees me," Skye said, softly, the way a wolf growls deep in its throat.

"Get him away from me! What's going on?" Mr. Grove's voice rose to a childish squeal. "He's not real . . . is he? But I haven't had a drink! I-I can't—"

"So tell me," Skye interrupted him. "Go ahead and tell me how nobody can prove anything, and therefore I'm not really dead."

Dusty's father had gone fish-belly pale. Backed into a corner, he could not move. "It can't be D.T.s," he whispered. "What is it?"

"Judgment," Skye said.

"Dusty." Her father's glance shot to her, panicked. "Dusty! You see him too? Help me!"

She said, "Just tell the truth for once." Skye had not yet raised his hands. If he did, Dusty did not know what she was going to do. Get between him and her father, maybe. Plead with him. But she hoped something else would happen. She still hoped Skye would somehow get past this himself.

She had given up hoping for her father.

"I did it for you, Dusty!" His gray, frightened stare clung to her.

Her mouth came open soundlessly, for she could not understand what her father was saying, not at all. Skye must have felt much the same way; he said, "*What?*" But her father looked only at her, not at Skye.

"I did it for you. I just wanted . . . I just wanted people to keep out. I just meant to scare them. That cable—" Amos Grove stopped and swallowed hard, darting a glance at Skye; then his gaze veered back to Dusty and begged her to understand as he went on. "I thought—I thought maybe it would dump a kid on his butt. You know you fell on that trail a hundred times and never got hurt. I never meant to hurt anybody."

Skye growled like distant thunder. "So you did put it there. You admit it."

"I admit it." Amos Grove faced him for a moment—but only for a moment. Then he had to look at the floor.

Dusty still did not get it; how could he have

thought he was helping her? "What do you mean, you did it for me?"

"Because of . . . because of what happened!" He stared at her as if she ought to know this. "If you couldn't ride out there anymore, nobody was going to."

She began to comprehend. It had started after the accident. "You never told me," she said, her voice low because she was starting to feel for him again.

"I-I couldn't talk about it. But I felt so bad—you, not able to get on that horse, go cantering up those trails—I had to do something."

Being at fault was the one thing her father had never been able to handle. And he knew the accident was his fault. Guilt had made him stop drinking for a while. But guilt had also made him do this terrible thing.

Dusty told him, "If you'd said something to me, I would have told you no, don't do it. You knew it was wrong."

"I-I didn't mean for somebody to get killed—"

"You had to know somebody could get hurt. Those ditches with nails in them—"

"They were just meant to blow tires out!"

"What if somebody stepped in one? You knew it could happen. And the cable—"

"I never meant—"

Skye took a step toward him, then stood like carved ivory with a silver sheen of rage. Skye spoke very softly. Too softly. "I'm just as dead whether you meant it or not."

Amos Grove stared at him, rigid, and didn't answer.

"Dad," Dusty appealed, "deal with it!"

His face, stretched with fright, tightened and settled into grim quietude. He nodded. Accepting. Finding some courage. With only a small hesitation he said, "I'll go to the magistrate in the morning. Give myself up."

All Dusty could do was look at him. The room got misty. She felt herself smiling. He was back. Finally her father, her capital-D Daddy, the Daddy she could depend on, was back.

He said, "Shoot, why wait until morning? Jail can't be any worse than the hell I've been going through. I'll call the cops now." He straightened, pushed himself away from the wall, and took a couple of shaky steps toward the phone.

But Skye blocked his path. "I will say what you will do or not do."

"Skye, let him go." Dusty felt a chill of fear. "He's—he's going to face up to it, don't you see?"

Skye didn't turn to look at her. Instead, he stepped closer to her father, poised like a sword, like a burning saber of rage, glaring. White fire pulsed and flared in him. "So you'll get, what, a few years in prison? A few months on probation? Not good enough. I'm not dead for a few years or a few months. I'm dead for all eternity."

Mr. Grove said, "I-I know. I've run out of excuses. There's no excuse." He faced Skye, and his voice quavered. "All I can say is—I'm sorry."

"Sorry's not good enough." Skye raised his hand. White flames flickered at his fingertips.

"Skye, *no!*" Dusty leaped to stand between him and her father, but then for a moment she couldn't speak. Her back hurt too much. And she was too . . . afraid.

"Get out of the way!" Skye's yell was a banshee shriek. His contorted face menaced, specter pale, sneering. It was hard to believe he had ever been beautiful. His fury was turning him into something ugly. Evil. A ghoul.

Forcing words past her pain and fear, Dusty said, "Even if you killed my father, he'd be better off than you are right now."

"Move! Or I'll take you, too!"

"Dusty, get out of here," her father whispered. She shook her head.

"Dusty, go! Get away! Let him have me."

"No!" She stood thinking feverishly; how could she break through Skye's rage? She said, "Skye. So you're dead, what's the big deal?"

"Get out or I will *show* you what's the big deal!"

Her belly went watery, she felt sick with terror, but she tried not to show it. "No, Skye, listen, I mean it. What's the problem? Okay, you're dead, but you're standing up, moving around—"

"Are you crazy?!" he screamed. His hair seemed to have turned to black fire. His eyes blazed red.

"Yes. I mean, no. I don't understand. Explain it to me. What's so bad about being dead?"

"You jerk, I can't feel anything!"

All his anger was for her now. As if he'd almost forgotten about her father. Good. Good. Dusty kept pushing it. "Like what? You can't feel walls when you walk through them? You can't turn doorknobs, so what?"

"Not like that, idiot! I can't feel anything *good*. I can't feel wind, or bike roar, or grass when I lie on it, or . . . or smell the road heat, the leaves, the trees, anything." His fiery, upraised hands menaced her—but then they wavered in the air like windblown birds. "I can't smell sunshine. Or a new car. Or food. I can't remember what a cheeseburger tastes like. Or pizza. Or cake and ice cream." Still vehement, his voice shuddered. Sadness jostled with his anger now. "Nothing seems real except Tazz, and he can't talk. I—there's nobody to talk with. My friends can't see me. Nobody sees me."

"I see you."

"You—you're a special case."

"I told your mother about you."

"So what? She can't even tell when I'm there. I went . . . I went to the house, but—they can't see me at all."

The fire leached out of Skye like lightning draining away into rain. His stance went dull; his head sagged. His hands drifted down to his sides, no fiercer than fog.

He said, "I can't bear it. They're . . . crying."

He was just a boy standing there, dim and gray and wretched.

"Skye . . ." Dusty stretched her hand toward him.

"Damn it." He closed his eyes hard and turned his face away.

"Skye, they love you. Look, you've been going around made of nothing but anger, you couldn't feel how much they love you—"

"Stop it," he whispered. His lidded eyes winced. His hands faltered up to cover his face.

Dusty did not stop. "If I'd known you—if I'd known you when you were alive, I think I would have loved you, too."

"Dusty, please stop." He could barely speak.

"I think I do love you." Her voice had dropped to a whisper, because it was a truth like a silver sword. "I think I do. I cry, too."

His shoulders clenched like a fist. He stood there with his head bowed, quivering. Dusty knew he could not see her hands lifting toward him.

"I've been there. Grief, I mean. I know what your family is going through."

He flinched and lowered his head even more. Dusty ached to have mercy on him and shut up. But she could not. Her father still stood behind her, pressed against the wall, white-faced, panting—and Skye could still kill him with a touch.

She said, "Skye—when I go to see your mom, what do you want me to tell her?"

He did not answer.

"Do you want me to tell her you've turned into a ghoul?" Dusty could not quite keep her voice steady. "Do you want me to tell her that you've had your revenge, you—you killed my father—"

"Shut up! I hate you, I hate you, I hate you!" Skye's hands flew down from his face, he crouched like a fighter, his fists curled at his sides, he glared white fire daggers at her. He shouted, and his voice broke like a heart.

"Goddammit, you can keep your father, okay?"

He spun away from her and ran.

Chapter Eight

Skye ran out of the house, straight through the closed door.

For maybe three heartbeats, Dusty stood in a great stillness broken only by her father's ragged breathing. Then she ran, limping, to the door, pulled it open, and headed out after Skye.

Dark out there. Shadows, dim stars, moonlight, a charcoal-and-white-ashes night like that first night when he had come to help her, when her heart was breaking because of Tazz and she had turned around to see him standing like a white marble Michaelangelo in Levi jeans at the stable door.

There he stood.

Not far from the house, with his horse—he had

run to Tazz just the way she used to. As muted and gray as rain, he stood with his arms around Tazz's neck, his face hidden in Tazz's mane. Dusty saw him quaking, saw his shoulders heave.

She had to be merciless just a moment longer. "Do you mean it?" she demanded, walking toward him.

His head jerked up and he whirled to yell at her; she saw the wet sheen of his beautiful face. "Of course I mean it!" Tears and fury in his voice. "Would you . . ."

Go away and let him alone, probably. But her chest swelled, aching like sunrise, and before he could say anything more, she took one more step and put her arms around him, crying as hard as he was.

Crying for her father, crying for herself, her own pain, her own death someday—but mostly crying for Skye. Weeping with relief and sadness and love of him, she hugged him and laid her head on his shoulder. Or on what looked like his shoulder—there was nothing there, she could feel no solid body, she might as well have been embracing air. But she could see him turn to her. She could hear him sob deep in his throat, see his shoulder tremble. She could see his arms come up around her to enfold her, though she could not feel the touch of his hands on her back.

Did he love her, too? Maybe he loved her, too—but she didn't know, probably she would never know, and the thought made her sob harder. And with every breath, her back hurt. Her stupid back hurt from crying. Damn, why did everything have to hurt so much? Oh, Skye. She could see his black hair, his bowed head. She could see the wet spot where her tears had soaked his shirt.

She could see . . . rising from where her tears had touched his back and shoulder, a white dawning so bright it made her close her eyes.

She gasped. For a moment everything seemed to stop—her tears, her breathing, her heartbeat, the night breeze, the voices of spring peepers from the pond, the whispering of trees, the slow, distant wheeling of stars, everything paused, caught up in a feeling of—not fear, exactly.

Awe.

Awe of the whiteness that aspired so bright it burned its way into her even through her lidded eyes. For a moment she could not move. But she could feel—

She gasped again. Glory. Wonder.

Healing.

She felt it running through her like spring water—and in that moment everything began anew, her breath, the moonlit breeze, the song of spring in breeze and pond and trees, her heart's warm drumming, her life. Wellness flooded her from Skye's hands, straightening her back, lifting her shoulders like wings, giving her strength and wholeness to run, leap, shout, ride wild horses. Joy warmed away her tears. Her eyes snapped open. She cried, "Skye!" She flung her head up to cry the miracle to him. "Skye, my back!"

But she stood openmouthed, and slowly, as if on their own, her hands released him. She stepped back, for his face, gazing gravely at her, was the starlight face of an angel.

He was . . . he was the texture of moon halo, he was indigo infinity and the glimmer of distant galaxies standing there. He seemed made all of starlight now, a misty constellation with shining eyes. And from his back rose great moon-white wings.

"It'll stay healed this time," he said. His voice was low, as always, gruff, as always, yet different. A warm trail winding through springtime woods. A red hawk flying. A hearth fire quietly talking.

Dusty couldn't speak. He gazed at her for a moment with just a wisp of a smile, and then his gaze floated away from her like a white moth, past her and upward, far away. His voice was husky, almost a whisper, as he broke the silence. "Well," he said, "I'd better get going," and for a moment she heard the kid in him again, trying to sound casual even though the words quivered with eagerness like his horse's pricked ears.

Tazz stood waiting, a silky shadow in the night. Skye turned to him and vaulted onto his back, starlight riding a shadow, wings rising high and white against the sky. With one hand he patted the horse's shoulder.

Looking down at Dusty he asked, "Tell my mom I'm okay?" ·

She nodded.

"Thank you, Destiny. Thanks for my wings. Thank you for everything."

He looked upward. Then his wings cupped and seemed to catch a rush of wind she could not feel. Tazz felt it, too; he arched his lovely neck and whinnied and lifted his forefeet into an easy leap and went cantering up the sky as if he were skylarking up a dark meadow thick with starflowers. Dusty stood watching Tazz running to the Milky Way, watching Skye ride. At first she could see Skye's rapt face, the arrow-straight lines of his arms and back and shoulders as he rode. She could see Tazz tucking his chin and snorting like a colt. Then she lost sight of the horse in the stardark, she could see only those great wings, and Skye seemed to be a white swan flying. Then he was a white comet in the night. Then a bright star.

Dusty got her mouth moving at last. "Thank you," she whispered. He was far away, but she knew he heard her, even . . . even in eternity, whatever it was like. She whispered, "If you see my mother, tell her I'm all right too, would you, Skye?"

"Well," Dusty told Katelyn in homeroom, "I got to stay in a foster home last night."

"*What?*" Katelyn stared. Katelyn was wearing frosted lilac eyeshadow that matched her frosted lilac fingernails but not her brown eyes.

"You didn't hear? I bet it was in the papers this morning."

"Like I read the newspaper?"

"Don't you listen to the news either?"

"Not in the morning! I'm doing good if I can stand upright in the morning." Although she'd managed to get her makeup on, obviously. "What happened? Your father—" Katelyn stopped short.

Dusty had long since forgiven Katelyn for speaking the simple truth about what had happened to Skye. "Daddy confessed," Dusty said as cheerfully as if she were talking about new shoes. "He spent the night in jail."

Katelyn peered at her, and no wonder. Dusty knew she shouldn't be smiling, but she couldn't help it. It was so good to be well again. No pain in her back. None. She felt well and strong enough to handle anything, even what might happen to her father. "He's out on bail now," she added. "He's home." And he was smiling, too. When she'd left for school, he had been sitting at the kitchen table, stark sober, watching her sashay out the door and looking like he wanted either to cry or to sing hallelujah.

Katelyn was still staring at her. "I don't get it. Why are you not totally freaked?"

"I . . . I'm just really relieved." Dusty couldn't tell Katelyn about her back, because that would have meant telling Katelyn about Skye, and Katelyn wouldn't understand. Katelyn was the kind of person who was good with people but not spirits. "I'm glad it's over," Dusty added, her words sounding lame even to her. It wasn't over yet. Daddy had to stand trial. He might go to prison.

"I don't care," Daddy had said to her, his eyes alight. "Just so you're all right, I'm the luckiest guy alive, and I don't deserve it. Your back is really okay? Really?"

"Daddy started to get himself a drink," she told Katelyn, "but then he threw it down the sink."

"Don't expect that to last." Katelyn was tapping her pale purple fingernails on the desk.

"My back's feeling better," Dusty blurted.

"That's good." Katelyn was not impressed. "Does your father have a good lawyer? Don't answer the phone when you get home. If it's in the paper, you're going to get hate calls."

Katelyn was just trying to help, Dusty knew. But there was too much that Katelyn did not understand, had not experienced and therefore could not possibly understand, no matter how hard she tried. With a pang, Dusty realized that Katelyn was no longer her best friend.

An angel was. An angel she would probably never see again.

Dear Diary,

Saturday. I went to see the Ryders today and told them all about Skye. I tried to explain what it was like when he got his wings. And when he rode Tazz up to the stars. I tried to show it to them, but I don't know if I can ever tell anybody what it meant to me to see that. I think that all the rest of my life, whenever anything seems too hard or too scary I will just think of that angel boy on horseback, riding up that dark sky trail, and I will be okay. It's a blessing that will never leave me that I was able to see that.

Good-bye, Skye. Smile down on me sometimes.

Good-bye, Tazz. I miss you, but I'm glad you're strong and well now, like I am.

I feel all the way alive now, right to my bones. These past couple of years I thought I was living, but I wasn't, not really.

In my heart I felt like it was all over for me, I just wanted to lie down and stay that way. But now that Skye touched me I feel like it's all just beginning. Funny that a dead boy should give my life back to me, but . . . It's weird, but it feels good. Like I do. Just plain good. Like I want to go out and eat cheeseburgers, and pizza, and cake with ice cream.

And go riding. Tazz was the best horse ever, but still—there's a whole world of other horses out there.

It was October, one of those blue-and-gold October days when you knew winter was coming but it didn't matter, and Dusty was out riding on her new horse, a tall gray thoroughbred mare named Dawn Treader. Her best friend rode with her on one of the chestnut mares, and her best friend was Skye's brother Canyon.

"This is pretty cool," he said, the hush in his voice telling her that he was seeing the same things she was: that the woods trail was a dream of silver-yellow aspen; that the gate was gone, the ditches filled in and overgrown with wildflowers, the scars almost healed on the hemlocks; that the sky was as blue and deep as the blue fire in Tazz's eyes the night Tazz had run to the stars. "It's no wonder Skye liked this," Canyon said. The trail, he meant. Or maybe he meant being on a horse. It was the first time he had ridden the trail on horseback, his head eight feet above the ground.

"He rode like he absolutely loved it," Dusty said.

They followed the path through the fringes of the woods, into a meadow wild with scarlet sumac, blackberry sprawls, purple fall flowers in yellow sunlight. Ahead lay soft trail running gently uphill. "Want to canter?" Dusty asked.

"Sure!" Canyon leaned forward like a young hawk spreading its wings.

She cantered a little behind him, watching him, feeling a lump in her throat: He was so handsome. Most of the time she saw him for who he was, Canyon, her buddy—but today, riding, with his face lifted to the wind that way, he looked just like Skye.

"Hot dog!" she yelled at him.

At the top of the rise they slowed to a walk again. Canyon was smiling, his head high, the color riding high in his cheeks.

"Feeling groovy?" Dusty kidded him.

"Huh?"

"Never mind." What a glorious day. Just because it was another reason to be glad, Dusty said, "Dad called me today." Her father had been sentenced and was serving his jail term, but on a work-release program so that he could continue to support his daughter and she could stay in their home. "He said, 'You know what day this is?' It's been six months since he's had a drink.''

Canyon nodded. "Six months since Skye died.''

As suddenly as the weather changing, life was serious—yet Dusty knew he hadn't said it to be mean. There wasn't any meanness in Canyon. He had something on his mind.

The horses swished through late daisies and asters. Down below, the darkwater pond threw off sparkles like stars. Dusty rode in silence, waiting.

Canyon asked, "You ever talk with spirits anymore?''

She wasn't expecting that. It spooked her. "Um, no. Why would I?''

"I don't know. I just . . . Listen, I just want you to know it never seemed weird to me. I mean, even the very first time I met you, I believed you. It makes sense to me that there would be . . . you know, angels and stuff.''

This wasn't like Canyon. He didn't usually talk much. Dusty's mare swerved to a halt as she peered at him. "Something got you thinking about Skye?''

He stopped his horse and looked at her. The only sounds were a lark calling, a horse stamping, late summer bugs talking in the tall grass.

"Canyon, spit it out. What's happened?''

He sighed, then asked her very quietly, "Did you

hear about that little girl who was lost out west? Out in Glacier Park?"

"No."

This was it, this was what was riding heavy in him, she could tell by his intense stillness as he faced her over his horse's ears. "There was an article in the city paper. Mom showed it to me. Little girl three years old, wandered off, and she was missing for days, they gave up on her, but here she came toddling up to a ranger station. She said an angel came and rescued her and gave her a horsie ride out of the woods. An angel on horseback."

Everything seemed to stop for a moment. Dusty could not hear the summer bugs. She could not feel Dawn Treader breathing under her.

"Huh!" she managed to say.

"Of course, nobody's paying any attention to her. It's just a cute story. Maybe she dreamed something. She's just a little kid."

The world rustled back to life as Dusty got herself and Dawn Treader moving again, lifting her head to look to the sky. She saw a butterfly rising like an orange spark. She saw a hawk soaring. Off in the distance, thunderheads billowed.

Riding beside her, Canyon said, "But I keep thinking, maybe we'll see him again sometime."

Dusty nodded. "Maybe," she whispered, scanning the sky.

Epilogue

Daily SouLog Anno Domini 1998, 10th moon, 24th day
Subject Skye Ryder, novice, effectively handled transition but is now restless and in need of challenge and activity. Subject volunteered for guardian angel duty but is not sufficiently disciplined; would he be steady enough to mentor a child from the moment of conception through transition? Doubtful. Subject assigned to border patrol and appears gallantly willing though somewhat impulsive and reckless. Intervention on behalf of very young human cannot be faulted, but did he have to manifest? Horsie ride undoubtedly comforting to the child, but perhaps unwise? Question arises whether horse should be equipped with wings as well. Animal appears loyal to novice and he to it. Maintaining watchful supervision. J. G., Sector Supervisor